FERTILE CLAY & ATTIC DUST

RUSSELL E. MAUER

iUniverse, Inc.

New York   Bloomington

FERTILE CLAY & ATTIC DUST

iUniverse books may be ordered through booksellers or by contacting:

iUniverse
1663 Liberty Drive
Bloomington, IN 47403
www.iuniverse.com
1-800-Authors (1-800-288-4677)

ISBN: 978-1-4401-7143-7 (pbk)
ISBN: 978-1-4401-7144-4 (ebk)

Printed in the United States of America

iUniverse rev. date: 2/10/2010

DEDICATION

I dedicate this book to my wife, Dorothy, for her love and understanding. She was a guiding influence in the journey from the way my life was to the way it has become.

I had a dream in which my granddaughter asked, "Are you going to leave me your fortune?" I replied, "Not if I can spend it all before I die." After a period of wakeful thinking, I realized that that was not true.

There are many kinds of fortune. My greatest fortune, I cannot spend. I have been blessed with a lot of happy hours, some of which I describe in these pages. These I leave to you, Michelle, my beautiful granddaughter, along with love, happiness, laughter, and joy.

CONTENTS

CHILDHOOD *The Way It Was*

SENIOR CITIZEN *After the Way It Was*

*Poems originally published in A Life's Essence by Russell E. Mauer

ACKNOWLEDGMENTS

My thanks to Mom and Dad, who contributed a work and social environment, which gave me the life, I refer to, as "you never had it so good."

Thanks to Aunt Cassie, Uncle Cliff and Cousin Edna who contributed some of their recollections. Many thanks to the writer's group, Authors Echoes, whose critiques were always appropriate and encouraging, and to Frances Porter and Ann Anderson whose comments and polish helped make the words flow reasonably.

PROLOGUE

Fertile Clay and Attic Dust relates stories from my family history and childhood that depict the "way it was." Some events from my life as a senior citizen illustrate something of the "way it is."

I experienced the Great Depression on a dairy farm in central Wisconsin in a Norwegian community called Suldal. It was named after a region by that name in Norway. The Norse ethic – religious to a fault, ready with a helping hand, and easily amused – was prevalent.

Mother's intellectual interests gave me an appreciation of animal life (wild and domestic). Father's gregarious personality, while not transferred to me, had a profound influence. I appreciated his views of life.

Sadly, many of the farming methods and customs of my childhood have disappeared. These are some of the valued memories of my early life that I now must pay money to see demonstrated at farm-days and state fairs. Hollywood also uses these same scenes to portray the early 20th century. Seeing reenactments of the old methods pleases me in a warm, nostalgic way.

DO YOU REMEMBER

Drove up north the other day
to see the old home town.
A couple uncles, one sweet aunt
and some cousins are still around.
Got to talking of old times,
they aren't that long ago.
Couldn't even recognize
some places I used to know.
They tell of flocks of wild turkey,
never heard of them in my day,
And deer frequent the very fields
where I used to put up hay.
Every year hunters harvest
in bluffs I used to roam.
It may have changed but sure as hell,
it's the place I still call home.
The creek I used to fish
where watercress grew wild,
Wonder if I'd recognize
things seen there as a child?
I've got to go back to that stream,

see if its course has changed,
Is that shallow wide spot there
where the cattle drank and ranged?
The "holes" I know, have disappeared,
eroded by many floods.
How many snaking "ox bows"
have given way to nature's muds?
That stream is still spring fed;
cold and crystal clear,
I've got to go and see if it
still brings that special cheer.

You know, I'd like to take you there,
relive my early childhood.
Show you what I mean when I say
"You never had it so good."

BEGINNINGS

One day, Elmer, a respected established young farmer, came to town and dropped off some plow shares for sharpening at the blacksmith shop. He remarked to Art, the blacksmith, "If you hear of anyone needing a job, send him out my way. I need a hired man. A young fellow down the road from me came looking for a job. I gave him a try hauling manure, but he left after half a day. Said he couldn't stand the smell."

By 1910, Ed, at age twelve, had received all his formal schooling. After his dad and mother died, he stayed with his brother Art, the blacksmith, gaining valuable experience helping in the shop.

Art told Ed about Elmer's comments, and the next day Ed walked into Elmer's yard with all he owned in a gunnysack over his shoulder asking for that job. Elmer said, "You've got enough ambition to walk all the way out here from town. That's good enough for me."

Gladys was Mabel and Elmer's first daughter born in 1901. The Lone Rock grade school stood on the fence line of the farm, a short walk from the house. The schoolteacher boarded with them, and convinced Mabel to send Gladys to school when she was four years old. She was sixteen when she graduated from high school.

By that time, she had four sisters who all learned how to handle a pitchfork as well as a broom. After two years working with her dad on the farm, Gladys went back to school attending La Crosse Normal working towards a teaching degree. During the second year, Mabel got sick, and Gladys had to drop out of college to help take care of her younger sisters.

Ed worked hard for Elmer and soon became the "son" he never had. He also assumed the role of "big brother" for the five daughters.

DANCING ON THE FARM

Life in the Lone Rock community was the usual never-ending farm work. Community entertainment was a good old country dance. Dances were held in a host farmhouse. With a room or two cleared, shaved wax sprinkled on the floor and chores finished, the music started. An accordion, a fiddle and whatever else was available provided the music and rhythms for the polka, waltz, one-step, two-step, sometimes a square dance or any other request.

Ed bought a fiddle cheap at an auction and taught himself to play. His new craft earned him a little money playing at dances, where they passed the hat. He gave that up when he found it was more fun to do the dancing than to provide the tunes.

Dances were especially entertaining for the young people. The floor was always crowded. With five daughters and a young hired man, Mabel and Elmer sponsored many a dance.

The dance floor was a place for young people to get better acquainted under the watchful eye of parents. The occasion could be something like the 4th of July, but usually a dance was initiated by someone, tired of all work and no play.

Everyone got out on the floor. Some of the married men enjoyed talking more than dancing, and after a waltz or two, found a space in the corner out of sight of their wives to swap stories. Wives when they gave up on their gossiping men, danced together with unprecedented liveliness. The muggy hot summer nights made perspiration flow—which made intermission a rush to the open windows or porch.

Young children had their own dances and games, sometimes organized, but more often spontaneous. The younger ones ran around amongst the dancers, nearly getting run over or stepped on. Once in a while parents would grab their child and waltz them in their arms.

Each family brought a dessert: cookies, cake or pie. Homemade lemonade was the main drink. When the dance was over, people who came by horse and buggy often gave old "Dobbin" his head while they slept all the way home. Sometimes Elmer's daughters made it home just in time to start the morning milking.

With his outgoing personality, Ed was quite the eligible bachelor, and had his pick of partners. Sometimes he didn't even need a partner, performing a jig out on the middle of the floor by himself.

One day, Ed and two friends climbed to the top of Lone Rock, the skyscraper sandstone formation at the back of Elmer's barn. The dance the night before was still warming their blood. "Ed, why don't you serenade the girls? I bet if you sang, *Molly Get Your Slippers On*, they'd come outside."

"You're on boys, but you've got to sing too. All together now."

"Come all you rounders if you want to flirt
For here comes Molly in her hobble skirt.
You can hug her if you want to,
You can kiss her if you please,
But you'll never get her hobble up above her knees. "

The five sisters all came rushing out of the house cheering the boys on. It was quite a show. They urged them to sing more, and when the serenading finished, invited them down for lemonade.

I can't imagine Dad singing, let alone singing that ribald melody but that's how Aunt Cassie remembers it. I do remember hearing a voice coming from the old tractor way up by the woods one time many, many years later. I'm sure Dad didn't realize the house could hear him singing over the tractor's noisy clatter.

By the mid 1920's, Ed and Gladys was a popular couple on and off the dance floor. Other eligible young women may have pursued Ed, but Gladys was the one he went home with. They married in 1928, and leased a farm in the Lone Rock community. Bob and I were born on that farm.

As the first-born grandchild, I became the center of attention for a while at the grandparent's farm. A swing attached in the doorway between the kitchen and living room entertained me for hours. When I tired of that, Granddad, sitting with his legs crossed, balanced me on his foot and bounced me up and down like on a teeter-totter. The house was always warm and cozy with family activity.

Dad shot a deer in the 1931 deer-hunting season. It hung on a branch of an oak tree in the yard to be skinned and cut into portions. Venison was a welcome addition to the meat larder in those days. Mom bottled a good share for those mincemeat pies she brought to the dances.

One particular dance was held on a fateful 4th of July. Plenty of fireworks were exploding on the lawn so the children spent most of their time outside. Meanwhile, a barn two or three miles away caught fire. I could see the flames as they pierced the darkness and felt horrified at the sight. Nightmares disturbed my sleep for a spell after that. Spontaneous combustion in those days was a result of putting too much damp hay in the barn.

After three years leasing, we bought a farm in Suldal valley, immediately west of the Lone Rock community. Some of the Lone Rock social activities went with us, but only for a short time. The Suldal Lutheran community had a prudish, intolerant attitude towards dancing. It was the devil's handmaiden, they said, described as the vertical equivalent of an unmentionable horizontal activity.

The first year, we held a dance at the new farm in early August. All the social attachments to our Lone Rock friends were still intact. The house was full, but most everyone there came from the Lone Rock community. You might say it was a house-warming event. It was warm enough. At intermissions all the ventilation (wide open windows) was in full use.

Becoming involved with the Lutheran community implicitly meant we become members of the church and adopt their code. No more dances at our house! Social activity was limited to school picnics and church luncheons. Alcoholic beverage, devil's drink, was *verboten.*

THE SHIVAREE

A shivaree was a rural custom initiating newlyweds into the community. The object was this: after the lights went out at night, to wait just long enough for love making to get started, then a crowd would rouse the couple out of bed with all the noise they could muster.

Aunt Jessie and Uncle Delbert were married in 1937. I was ring bearer and cousin Edna was the flower girl. We practiced the night before. The wedding was uneventful. After the honeymoon, husband and wife came back to run the Lone Rock home farm.

Ed Brockup, a member of the community, had an old "Star" stock truck, which fit the noise bill for a shivaree. The crowd gathered at Milo's place next door. After the lights went out, Ed drove his truck into the driveway next to the newly wed's house. He proceeded to turn the switch off and on, off and on, which made it backfire with tremendous blasts. The rest of the crowd gathered in the yard, lighting firecrackers and banging pots and pans until the couple appeared. After some drinks and desserts, brought by women in the crowd, the party dissolved, and the newlyweds returned to their nuptials.

The house of another newly married couple in the Suldal community was on the hillside of a narrow valley. Their shivaree started with a big, big bang. Dad set off a stick of dynamite close by on the opposing hillside. That nearly rattled the shingles off their roof.

These were family or familiar customs, which served to keep things exciting. The form of awakening with loud blasts lends credence to the name for this event.

Shivaree.

THOSE SPOILED KIDS

Looking back on my life gives the general impression that "you never had it so good". My grandparents, Mabel and Elmer Niles, and my parents, Ed and Gladys, instilled in me that impression. I expect that my children will also have it when they become seniors.

The family history started in Wisconsin's Juneau County, on a dairy farm. Lone Rock was a massive five-acre bluff in the middle of flat farmland. That rock, (the community landmark) overshadowed Granddad's barn.

As a result of my being Mother's first born, I was nicknamed, Buster. A woman, pregnant for the first time, doesn't realize until it happens, how much an unborn child exercises its muscles. I was "christened", Buster, after I gave my first belly kick inside her womb. That has been my nickname in the family ever since.

Dad and Mother came to my college homecoming football game one year. Dad got to talking with some of the men, and happened to mention Russell, my proper name. It was so strange to my ears; I remember it to this day.

I returned home to a funeral after an absence of many years. One of my cousins asked me, "What do we call you?" I replied, "Anything but Buster and I wouldn't know who you are talking to." On the other hand, when another cousin's new husband called me Buster, it seemed almost an insult.

My brother, Bob, was two years younger than me. He was my fishing and hunting partner. We fished and hunted a lot together. He always seemed to catch the biggest and most fish. I, being the elder, rowed the boat or ran the motor. Two hunting incidents stand out. First, Bob shot his first deer, a fourteen-point buck, when he was twelve years old, and second, we both learned not to carry our guns cocked. Walking behind me one day, Bob's gun accidentally discharged, narrowly missing me. Our parents never heard about that incident.

Occasionally on a Sunday after church, my cousin Edna's family and the Mauer's family got together for lunch at either farm. We two, I, the first-born grandchild and Edna, the first-born granddaughter, got into things we maybe shouldn't have. We were explorers.

One Sunday afternoon, we discovered the attic at Edna's house. We found a stash of flapper clothing among other antiques. That inspired a regular costume party. We entertained the "old folks" all day with those strange clothes, particularly the gaudy hats. Edna's recall of this episode—one with pictures in strange frames—appears to come from a completely different attic than I remember.

Edna recalled another escapade where we laid a board across from the silo to the barn roof so we could crawl over.

We both got across and back. If I succeeded, she wasn't going to be out done. I dropped the board after she got down and it hit her on the head, not enough that we needed help, thankfully, but she may have suffered a headache afterwards. I have no recollection of the silo incident at all, but it would be something I would try. It does make me wonder, how did we ever live to retirement?

As kids, we two were probably quite the brats who got away with our "spoiled" behavior, but what is being first born for anyhow???

ANIMAL BEHAVIOR

For me, beginning life on a diversified dairy farm meant exposure to all kinds of livestock: chickens, pigs, sheep, and horses, not to mention dairy cows.

I watched calves being taught to drink from a bucket, chicks growing up in the brooder house, and sows nursing their piglets. Calves were stubborn about putting their muzzle down into a pail of milk, they had to be trained, chicks did everything without a mother to teach them, and pigs gourmandized their meals.

Most dairy cows were milked two times a day, every day of the year except for about a month just before calving when they had a vacation to get in shape for their new calf. All the milk went through the separator dividing it into cream and skim milk. Cream brought cash at the creamery and skim milk mixed with ground corn fattened the hogs and sometimes chickens raised for meat.

If you've seen hogs eat, especially ground corn mixed with skim milk, you know they delight in their food. As a toddler, I watched them greedily eat, and knew that had to be some good stuff filling their trough. The pigs grabbed a mouthful, tossed their heads back, and then swallowed in a hurry to gobble more till it disappeared. That made an impression on me.

One day Mother found me in the pigpen with the pigs trying to sample that good tasting ground corn and milk. Shocked, she said, "That slop is for the pigs!" as she pulled me out.

That ground corn and milk left a lasting impression. To this day, corn flakes with 2% milk is my favorite breakfast.

BUTTERFLIES

Cramped indoors, children can be mighty stressing wearing off their energy when the mother is preparing for visitors. Bob and I were being particularly stressing one early summer day. Mom had to get us outside to use up that energy.

White cabbage butterflies were invading her garden laying eggs on the cabbage. Her boys could help alleviate that problem.

"Boys, I'll give you a nickel for every white butterfly you bring me," she said.

We took off after those pests with the enthusiasm of four- and six-year-old farm kids. The butterflies were just out of reach; we chased one and then another—to no avail. Those elusive wings maneuvered just a little higher than our hands could reach. We needed a different approach. We tried sneaking up on them, but they seemed to have eyes in the back of their heads. Finally, approaching from a blind corner, we caught one and raced to the house to collect the bounty.

The rewarded nickel really whetted our appetites for more. Surely there had to be a better way to get those critters. A stick was too skinny, and a fly swatter too small to be effective. What if we combined stick and swatter – how about the branch off a lilac bush? I broke off a dead branch and went whipping away after a pest. It really worked. Bob got another branch and together we made life miserable for white butterflies in that garden. If we got close to one it didn't stand a chance. In short order, we reduced the butterfly population by five, and drove the rest out into the hay field. It was time to collect the reward.

That's when Mother learned it was too expensive to use money as enticement to get her boys motivated, she dropped the bounty to one cent.

Maybe there's no connection, but butterfly collecting for a college Entomology class helped make me a Biology major, which eventually earned me more than loose change.

THE SULDAL FARM COMMUNITY

A farm community, including the farm businesses in early to mid 20th century Wisconsin, was almost family. Many individuals were related directly, others by marriage, and the rest by church, school, and the party telephone.

Suldal was a typical diversified dairy farming area. It got its name from the early settlers who came from a place with the same name in Norway. Surrounded by bluffs on three sides, it reminded them of their homeland. Everyone worked in his own way, and got through the depression. Cows, chickens, pigs and gardens, along with horses, kept food on the table so no one starved.

The Norwegians spoke two languages into the thirties; many were more fluent in Norse than English. They were very clannish, even amongst themselves. East Valley Lutherans wouldn't go to Sunday church in the Suldal Valley church and vice versa, even though some lived closer to the other's church.

Little Herman was a fixture in the community. At one time or another, he worked for almost every farmer in the neighborhood. He loved and respected horses and was able to do more things with them than impatient and less understanding people could. He was a hard worker and excellent teamster. When they hired him, some tried to reform him since he was an alcoholic, but most accepted and respected Herman as he was.

Communities were usually defined by the school district. Walking distance from the school was about as far as farmers could drive the team and wagon and still have time to help their neighbors with threshing or silo filling.

Children growing up in these farm communities were initially introduced to other kids under the protection of the family home. Further exposure came at the homes of grandparents, aunts and uncles and possibly church. The first 6 years of my country boy's life were spent at home with Mom and Dad and younger brother, Bob. I enjoyed a somewhat hallowed position as first-born. Bob and I took a major step in separating the umbilical cord when we entered grade school. Here we mixed with unrelated kids with no parents to intercede. We made new friends and sometimes enemies. Relatives in school alleviated much of the stress.

The first week of school was humiliating for me. Too embarrassed to raise my hand to go to the outhouse, I wet my pants. I learned to live with the shyness and school became a joy.

Each farm district was quite self-reliant. If a cow had a calving problem, someone in the immediate area was often called before the veterinary. Community machinery was repaired and maintained within the neighborhood. Dad was one of the people looked to for much of this expertise. He kept the community machinery in repair, blades sharpened, and equipment greased. He and Uncle Art, the blacksmith in town, attached a circular saw to the front of our old tractor to cut wood into chunks to burn in the wood burning stoves. Sawing stove-wood was another community project. Dad, like most others, could be counted on if someone needed assistance.

The extent of the depression's influence on farming was expressed in the market for pork one year. An old sow was selected for market. Dad determined it would cost more to have her trucked to market than she would bring in cash so he gave her to a neighbor on the other side of the bluff. They were having a rough time of it. They were very thankful, claiming the hog was the main thing that got them through the winter that year.

The party telephone, in addition to improving communication, insured not much could happen in the neighborhood without everyone knowing about it. There were a few old maids whose soap opera of life was listening on the party line. It worked almost as well as 911 for emergencies.

School and church united the women in the community. They initiated projects such as the 4-H club, and organized kid's social and birthday parties. Finding games to keep the kids occupied was a challenge. Mom was a leader in school affairs and the 4-H club.

There was a cohesiveness about farm life that felt family-like. Unlike city life now days, neighbors knew each other by first name, and kept in touch without being too nosey.

HARVESTING HAY

Hay making methods in the 1930's were changing fast. In the old times, hay had been cut with a scythe, but now, with the advent of new farm machinery, it was cut with a mower pulled by a team of horses.

After the cut hay wilted, a large version of a garden rake—called a dump rake—was used to drag it into a row. This row of drying clover or alfalfa was then forked into cocks—piles of hay with the stems on the outside and thatched on top to shed any rain. From the cock, the hay was pitched onto the hay wagon, hauled to the barn or a haystack and unloaded. A side delivery rake would soon replace the dump rake. It rolled the wilted hay into a windrow, with the stems, the slowest drying part of the hay, on the outside. Afterward, the hay could be put into cocks for further drying, but a machine called a hay-loader could also be used with the windrow. Hitched behind the hay wagon straddling the windrow, the hay-loader picked up the dried hay and delivered it up to the man loading the wagon as it moved down the row.

Innovations to reduce leaf loss and increase nutritional value of this essential animal roughage were developing rapidly. Some older farmers were very skeptical about these new methods of making hay. Their main contention was that all of this machine-directed beating, kicking, and grabbing—especially when the hay was dry—led to loss of a lot of leaves, the main nutritional part of the hay.

A typical week of haying started with cutting enough for three wagonloads. It wilted a day before raking it up with the dump rake. Then it was piled in cocks to complete the drying. Without rain, it would be dry enough for the barn in three days from the day it was cut. Each day we cut at least three more loads. If hay was put in the barn too wet it could heat up to the point it spontaneously ignited and burned barn and all.

Haying the old way was a three-man job. Cutting, raking and cocking could be done by one person; but loading the wagon was three simultaneous separate jobs: pitching the hay onto the wagon, placing the hay properly around the load, and driving the team beside the row of cocks. Unloading at the barn also required three separate people: one to set the harpoon hay fork, another to spread the hay around evenly in the mow—the space in the barn hay was stored—and a third to drive the team to lift the hay off the hay rack, up and over to the mow.

One mid-season, Dad bought a new hayfork called a grapple-fork. It was designed to pick up the hay by anchoring in the corners of the section of the load to be lifted, rather than in the center as with the harpoon fork. It made it much easier to handle the hay, and also, to remove hay from the mow for feeding the cows in the winter.

Until I was old enough to drive the team, Dad needed extra help during haying season. Mother, if available, and Dad would fill two of the necessary positions, but during the harvest season, a hired man was needed. Little Herman, a local laborer, was the solution.

Herman fit the neck yoke around Dime's neck, strapped it closed, and threw on the harness. He repeated the procedure on Dick. The team was ready to make hay. By noon, the hay proved dry enough to start putting it in the barn.

I remember when I was six years old and assigned driving duty. I stood proudly behind the front standard and, holding the reins, steered the team beside the row of cocks, starting and stopping with my "Giddy-up" and "Whoa." Little Herman pitched the hay on to the hayrack, and Dad forked it around to balance the load. Loading in definite front and back sections allowed the hay to separate more easily when lifted to the mow. As the load got higher, I moved up the standard. When I reached the top, the wagon was full.

Dad took over the reins to drive to the barn. Now, off-duty, I stretched out in the middle of the load, and watched the cumulus clouds change shape in that chicory blue sky. This was dreamtime. As the wagon bounced along, cushioned on my mattress of hay, I imagined I was floating on a cloud.

When we arrived at the barn, the team pulled the wagon into the open door of the center mow. Herman unhooked them, and they walked singly out beside the load. Mom caught them and drove to the end of the barn, and hooked up to the doubletree attached to the hay rope.

With the trip rope, Dad pulled the hayfork along the track in the peak of the roof to the release mechanism right over the load of hay. This allowed the fork to come down to the load. He set the fork as deep into the hay as he could, and securely anchored the barbs and hollered, *okay.*

Mother drove the team towards the tobacco shed, lifting the hayfork loaded with hay up to the center catch on the track. The mechanism inserted into the carrier system and rolled towards one end of the barn. When it reached the proper mow, Herman hollered *okay* and Dad yanked the trip-rope, dropping the hay for Herman to spread around evenly. Mother drove the team back to the starting spot to wait for the next fork load to be pulled up, while Dad retrieved the hayfork to repeat the process.

After three wagon loads, it was time for chores, and haying stopped for the day.

The next day, if it looked like rain, we would start loading by ten. I remember one year when, by the second load, a big thunderhead was advancing from the west. When the third load was finally on, Dad hurried the team towards the barn. Fat raindrops were already starting to fall. In my dreamy spot in the middle of the load, I watched the approaching thunderhead. Suddenly, a wheel hit a big lump of clay just as the wagon turned towards the barn. The load was going to tip. "Whoa!" Dad hollered as the load rolled. I went over with it, hay sliding over my head. I started to shout and holler for someone to get me out. I came clawing out of that pile like a drowning man reaching for air. When I realized that all was well, my tears changed to laughter at how scared I had been. I thought the whole load was on top of me, but it was only a sprinkling of loose hay from the top of the load.

Dad cursed to himself, "That will teach me to chain the rack to the bolster. It never would have tipped if I had it tied down!" Since the cloud floated by, dropping most of its rain south of the farm, Dad and Herman hurried to reload the wagon before more rain came along.

Friday, haying was finished and Herman, his week's pay in his pocket, headed on foot for town. Dad knew he wouldn't see him again till the money was gone. Herman would live up to his reputation; he was a good worker—till payday.

On Monday morning, when Dad entered the barn to milk, he found Herman, sleeping by the horses. The man was all-apologies for his semi-inebriated condition. Since there was corn to cultivate that day, which required much walking, Herman would recover from his hangover in no time.

By the time the corn was all cultivated, a second crop of hay was ready to cut—and the haymaking process started over again. Ever since the hay toppling accident, Dad had the hayrack securely chained to the bolster. I too learned a lesson: instead of watching clouds, I watched the load—in case I had to abandon ship.

THOSE OLD PLUGS

I sat on the hay wagon directly behind two pair of monstrous bulging thigh muscles. That was power, horsepower, and the epitome of strength. This was my impression from the first time I sat there until those horses finally retired permanently to pasture.

Over the first half of the twentieth century, tractors gradually replaced the team of horses for providing horsepower on the farm. I spent my childhood during the end of this transition, from 1929 to 1950. Being mechanically minded, I favored the tractor, but Dad said, "We've got to feed those horses whether they work or not; that tractor coasts on idle." This philosophy helped make horses one of my least favored farm animals. Doing something with the team I could do with the tractor was not moving with the times.

Horses have a mind of their own, and consequently, personalities—some good, some bad. Castration usually eliminated most of their aggressiveness, but not all of their loco tendencies. Under control, they did a lot of work; but out of control, they could do a lot of damage. Influenced by a charge of adrenaline, all hell broke loose. Farmers called the result a run-away; a wild-eyed, out of control, all out stampede.

I grew up with Dick and Dime, a team of geldings, one black and one grey. Both were docile enough; but when Dime saw movement behind and over his head, he panicked, and took off running, and Dick went with him. Blinders on the bridle prevented some of this spooking, but not all. Dick and Dime were involved in a number of run-aways. I witnessed some of these. It did not improve my opinion of horses.

The last cutting of hay was in the barn. Dad hitched the team to the hay-loader to pull it to the tobacco shed for storage. "Giddy-up." The doubletree jingled as the team moved. Out of the corner of his eye, Dime saw the top of the hay-loader move, and bolted with Dick following to keep up. The reins jerked out of Dad's hands as the team headed for an open gate to the unused hog pasture. As they passed under a tree, branches caught in the upper slats breaking both slats and branches. The team slowed to a stop as they reached the fence at the end of the pasture. When Dad caught up with them, he profanely shouted, "No more grain for you two old plugs this month."

Silo filling had started. The team hitched to the corn-binder fitted with a bundle carrier stopped for a minor adjustment. The corn, a new hybrid, was especially tall. Over his blinders, Dime caught a glimpse of a tassel waving in the wind. Both horses bolted leaving a deep set of footprints in the moist earth. Bundles shot out on to the bundle carrier until it bent to the ground twisting back behind the binder.

Dad had a limited vocabulary of swear words, and used it liberally, cursing those old plugs, vowing he'd never cut corn with them again.

In the thirties, most of the corn was husked by hand in the field. The box wagon, fitted with a sideboard to catch the ears as they were tossed against it, moved down the row. The team started and stopped responding to Dad's "giddy-up" and "whoa." Both Mom and Dad worked together husking corn. Bob played in the front of the wagon while I tried my hand at husking.

Dad tossed one ear of corn with a particularly high arch. Dime saw it over his blinders, and took off with Dick, streaking towards the end of the field where they stopped. Mom and Dad raced to the wagon finding Bob crying, but unharmed by his bouncing ride. Dad's response, "That's it! We start looking for a new tractor tomorrow. The next time you two plugs pull anything, it will be the tractor stuck in the mud somewhere. I'd like to see you try to run away with it!"

Buster grinned!!!

TRACTORS

In the beginning of the twentieth century, steam engines, "Rumely OilPulls", and finally, gas powered precursors of the modern tractor provided power for belt driven machinery such as silo fillers, threshers, sawmills, etc. The combustible fuel for the steam engine was usually wood or coal. The "Rumely OilPull" used kerosene, and the modern tractor used gasoline or diesel. Steam power was for locomotives or stationary projects. The "OilPull" also worked best on a stationary project. The early gas or diesel-powered tractor was mobile enough to replace the team for many of the tilling operations, but was awkward for tight corners, and therefore, not always a good substitute for a team on the smaller valley farms. The tricycle wheel arrangement on a gas or diesel powered tractor increased its maneuverability.

Dad's brother, Hank, owned a "Rumely OilPull," which the Lone Rock neighborhood used for belt power on their community machinery. To me, it looked like a cross between a railroad locomotive and an army tank. The exhaust stack seemed as big as the cupola on the barn roof and as black as soot. Starting it in the morning was a chore, but there was no mistaking when it was going. I could hear its slow deep throated one cylinder whump---whump---whump on a quiet morning clear over in Suldal Valley, two or three miles away. Belt power was all it was good for.

Most gas powered vehicles in the thirties started by hand cranking. One had to be careful how he griped the crank handle because engines sometimes backfired. The thumb could be broken if it was wrapped around the handle. In the summer the tractor usually started easily, but in the winter with temperatures in the single digits, it was very difficult to crank the motor. Our tractor in the winter was used for belt power on a circular saw used to cut wood into chunks for the furnace and cooking stove. One winter, Dad had to put a fire under the oil pan to get things warm enough to start it.

Easy handling tractors with rubber tires and starters were on the way to take the place of these cumbersome giants.

THE FARMER AND THE SALESMEN

Farming in 1920's and 30's central Wisconsin dairy country was more horse sweat and elbow grease than gasoline smoke. Every farm had at least one team of workhorses. A few had a tractor, which took the place of the team for some tilling.

Tractors in the thirties were big lumbering, steel-wheeled, steel-lugged leviathans that left tracks like broad high-heeled shoes on soft dirt. They almost jarred my teeth loose when I sat on the fender riding over a hard surface.

Dad was a relatively modern farmer because he owned a 10-20 McCormick Deering tractor for plowing and discing. He still used the horses to plow small plots like the vegetable garden, walking in the furrow with the reins looped around his neck and shoulder. The horses were used for all the planting machinery.

By the end of the thirties tractors were changing drastically. The "row crop" tractor had evolved with the front wheels close together to complete the tricycle configuration. Rubber tires were the rule with batteries for starters on most models. Power could be supplied to the machinery directly by a power take-off on the tractor rather than through the turning of the machinery wheels.

Farm implement dealers at the end of the thirties carried in stock, a lot of advanced, and sometimes novel, tilling and harvesting equipment. They encouraged farmers to change some of their practices so they would buy their machinery.

In a neighborhood such as Suldal, a few farmers replaced their horses with a tractor, but many were afraid to try new ways until they saw them work; and tractors were expensive. Some older farmers who used horses as the sole source of power naturally felt more competent and confident with horses than tractors. Even though they realized they could do a lot more, and faster with the tractor, they stayed with their team of horses. Many of those who did get tractors kept the team around anyway. Their horses were part of the family.

As the depression receded, improved efficiency became a goal. A farmer could handle more land and more cattle with modern equipment. Replacing the team of horses with a modern tractor was basic to improving efficiency.

Tractor and equipment dealers around the valley saw these pressures for potential sales. Their livelihood depended on the farmer buying their product and this started with the tractor. When a farmer bought a tractor, he would generally buy his ancillary equipment at the same place when the time came. Initially farmers altered their horse equipment for use with the tractor, but eventually, those implements wore out and had to be replaced.

Kastner Implements made it through the depression by selling and repairing farm machinery in Mauston, the Juneau County seat. While not getting rich, the business maintained a franchise for Alice Chalmers tractors, which included a full line of equipment for both horse and tractor.

By discreet green manure fertilizing on some of the more depleted soil— planting sweet clover and plowing it under when it was lush—Dad was able to grow decent corn and oats on his tobacco leached farm. With the help of the team of geldings and the old "10-20", he kept the mortgage paid, and successfully survived the depression by working sixty acres of land. The remaining sixty acres of the farm was bluff timber and creek bottom.

By the late thirties the tractor was antiquated, even though the steel rims had been cut off and replaced with rims for rubber tires. Knobby tires replaced the steel lugs, and riding on the fender on a hard surfaced road no longer jarred the stuffing out of me. Traction wasn't as good as before, but that left room for the tire companies to experiment with new tread styles.

By 1940, it was apparent to Dad that the old tractor needed replacing, so he started looking at new ones. Kastner Implements was his first stop. Bill Kastner saw him looking at the shiny new Alice Chalmers "WD" on the lot and came over.

"Hi, Ed." He said to my father. "What do you think of the new model? This tractor can replace your team of horses just like that."

Dad countered, "I suppose it can, but without the horses, what will I pull the tractor out with when it gets stuck?"

"You thinking of buying a new tractor? I can give you the best deal around," Bill quipped encouragingly.

"Well, it seems to me this would be a good time to buy a new one if I can afford it. What does this one cost?"

"You should be able to afford this one, Ed. It pulls two sixteen-inch plows, and it's got plenty of power on the belt. It even has power take-off to use with your new hay mower."

"One thing at a time, Bill. Art, my brother, the blacksmith, can hook anything to the tractor I don't want to pull with the team."

"Are you going to trade in your old McCormick? I noticed that Art fixed it for rubber tires. I guess it runs a lot smoother now on those gravel roads."

"I can't see wasting space housing the old one if I've got another tractor around. What'll you give me on a trade-in? Really, all I'm interested in is the final price. It doesn't matter what you say this costs. My out of pocket is what I'm interested in."

"Why don't I come out to your farm tomorrow and look the old '10-20' over."

"That should be OK. I'll be around somewhere. Gladys can find me."

Dad left the shop, and drove to the creamery to pick up some buttermilk for the hogs. The price was right, free to farmers selling their milk to the creamery. It cost the creamery more to get rid of it then it was worth, and, mixed with ground corn, the hogs really did well on it.

As long as he was looking at tractors, Dad figured he'd run up to New Lisbon. Earl Peterson was getting into the farm implement business selling Massey Harris tractors. The Massey adds in the farm magazines looked inviting. Earl might give him a deal.

"Hi, Earl. I see you are getting into the farm machinery business. Do you have one of those new Masseys around?"

"Sure, Ed. Look at this "101 Junior" here in the shop. Steers and rides like a car. A nice two plow, forty on the belt, machine. It will cost you about $1,500 dollars."

"I've got a '10-20' McCormick Deering to trade in. I'm just interested in the difference."

"Why don't I come out tomorrow and look at your old tractor. I'll give you top price on your trade-in."

"Bill Kastner said he was coming out tomorrow to give his estimate. Maybe you'd better wait until the day after."

"Oh, your going to get us bidding against each other, are you?"

"Sounds like a good idea, but I really want to get the tractor that will do me the best job for the money. Every brand is coming out with this new row-crop design now. I need to see what's best for me so I'm looking around."

Bill came by the next day to check the "10-20". "Ed," he said to my father. "Looks like this old girl has seen better days. About all I can do with it is sell it for junk. It would make a pretty good pile for the Japs to melt down. I hear they're buying up a lot of it. Tell you what. You give me $1,200 dollars and I'll bring that new Alice out this afternoon."

"I bet you would," quips Dad. "Anyway, I've got some other tractors to look at. Earl Peterson is coming over tomorrow to give me a price on his Massey. I haven't seen the John Deere or the Ford yet either. I'd kind of like to see how they run before I buy."

"Tell you what I'll do, Ed. Why don't I bring that Alice out and let you try it for a week."

"Sounds like a good idea, but we're getting ready to fill silos. That will take up all my time for the next couple of weeks." They talk a while longer and Bill leaves.

What Bill said about bringing his tractor out for a demonstration got Dad to thinking. He really did need to see what all the dealers have to offer and how they compare. With silo filling coming up, it would be a good chance to test each one, especially if each dealer demonstrated his tractor at a different farm. All these dealers should jump at a chance to show off their product – and to the whole valley too.

The Alice Chalmers, Ford, John Deere, and McCormick dealers were located in Mauston. Although, not well known to Dad, he could at least talk to them. Three other dealers were some distance away. It wouldn't be easy to arrange a demonstration day on the phone with them. He discussed it with some of the neighbors in church Sunday, and, sure enough, some of them knew the far away dealers. They thought it was a great idea, and they all wanted to see the different tractors demonstrated on the silo filler. By week's end, seven dealers made arrangements to have their models in the valley to show off their power on the silo filler.

Silo filling started at our farm where both the Massey and the Alice were standing by ready to use—both shiny brand new models. Both Peterson and Kastner were there to see that everything was right with their tractors.

The farmers unloaded their wagons full speed with no trouble. But for me, the eleven-year-old, who was excited about these new tractors; that Massey sure was a lot easier to handle than the Alice. That "WD" had two hand brakes, one by each fender, and a hand clutch. It would be hard to handle if they all had to be used at once. But the bright red with yellow trim 101 Junior Massey Harris really caught my eye. Its manual controls handled just like a car. It got my vote right from the start.

The next farm was the Larson's, and the Ford tractor was on hand. Next to the Alice and the Massey, it looked like a toy, and it wasn't a tricycle type of wheel arrangement either. It did its job on the belt satisfactorily, but didn't stand much of a chance in the bidding competition in my eyes. Even the light gray color put me off.

At Tim Wright's place, the new deep red Farmall "H" made its appearance. It was almost a copy of the Massey, but the controls were much stiffer. It almost took a man to push the clutch in, as compared to the Massey. It did its job as expected, and the operation moved on to the next farm.

The green two-cylinder John Deere had its show at the Johnson's. This was the only tractor without an electric starter. It started fine by spinning that heavy flywheel, but you had to get off the tractor to do it, a real nuisance compared to just pushing the starter button. What was impressive was its slugging power. Even when it got pulled down in speed under a heavy load; where other tractors with more cylinders might be expected to stall, this tractor came back if you gave it half a chance. That heavy flywheel really did a job and impressed quite a few farmers.

Three dealers didn't have the models Dad wanted on hand, but got farmers with new tractors in nearby communities to come for a day. The dark green Oliver looked like the Massey Harris. The Minneapolis Moline looked more like our old "10-20" McCormick, and it was a bigger tractor than the rest; rated for three plows rather than two, which is all Dad figured he needed. The strange steering arm was all that I remember about the Case.

With silo filling finished, the bargaining began. All but the Alice Chalmer and the Massey Harris were quickly eliminated, mostly due to the personalities of the dealers. The John Deere and McCormick Deering were too high priced, with little encouragement to negotiate. The final bargaining came down to Kastner and Peterson. It was like an auction with the old "10-20" the object of the bidding, but they were not standing face to face, and Dad was the auctioneer.

Dad went to town one Wednesday in September when the weather was too miserable to do any corn husking. He stopped at the Kastner Implement dealer first. Bill came over right away.

"Morning, Ed. Have you come to close the deal on that Alice?"

"I'm going to buy a tractor, Bill, but I'm a long way from closing the deal. I see there's a two-row cultivator that fits on that Alice. How does that work?"

"It's a handy rig, Ed. Fits right on the back and hooks up to the power-lift. Just kick the lever and it comes right up. Does a real nice job with either springs or shovels. We can put one on so you can see for yourself how it works."

"Would you do that, Bill? I've got some other business in town so I'll go do that and come back later."

"Give us about an hour, and we should have it in place."

Dad headed for the bank, but decided to drop in at the blacksmith, just around the corner from the bank. When he got his new tractor, there would be a few things that might require Art's help; like adjusting wagon tongues to use with the tractor rather than with the horses.

"Hi, Art. It looks like everybody's got a couple plowshares in for repair. Some of these look like they're almost beyond hope."

"Hi, Ed. Those guys in the sand don't take long to wear them down. They figure it's cheaper to put on a new point and build out that edge than to buy a new one. I put them on and they seem to do the job. Keeps me busy anyway. What are you doing in town? It must be important to be here the middle of the week."

"I came in to deal on a new tractor with Kastner. We had a bunch of dealers demonstrate their tractors on the silo filler last month, and I've got to decide what I can afford, and which one to get. Bill seems to want to deal, but he doesn't have the best product in my eyes. When I get a new tractor I'll probably need your help altering some machinery to use with it. For one thing, that wood-saw you hooked up to the front of the old "10-20" will need some fancy adjusting to make it work with the new tractor."

"Just bring it around when you get ready, and I'll see what I can do." They talked family talk for a while before Dad left for the bank. At the teller window, he asked to speak to John. John waved him into his office.

"I haven't seen you for a while, Ed. How are things out in the valley? You seem to be prospering."

"I guess I can't complain, but I'm in need of a new tractor, and thought I'd better come in and see what I can afford. I've got an old "10-20" McCormick for trade-in and a few dollars saved to boot. I'll probably need $500 at least to make the deal."

"Things are looking up around the county. Quite a few farmers are thinking along those lines. I don't see any reason for any problem with that, Ed. With the economy starting to pick up again it seems like a good idea to modernize. Go ahead and make your deal. I'm sure we can handle your loan."

"Thanks, John. I wouldn't want to get tied up in something I couldn't handle. By the way, the boys seem to be catching some pretty good brook trout in the creek. They seem to know where they're at."

"Thanks, Ed. I'll keep that in mind some afternoon."

Dad headed back to Kastner's and found them still working on the cultivator. Bill called him over to his office for coffee, and showed him some literature on new equipment he was getting in.

"I'm handling the 'New Idea' line of equipment now. They're coming out with a lot that you'll be thinking of buying soon. Look at this hay-loader. With this tight bottom it won't loose nearly as many leaves as some of the others. It hooks on behind the wagon, and runs that windrow right up to the top of the load.

"I've already got a hay-loader, Bill. They had one at an auction over in South Valley. I probably paid too much for it, but I thought it would save enough time to make it worth it. Elmer thought it was the worst idea I'd had in a long time. He just can't go along with the new labor saving equipment coming out in farming these days. He thinks we're wasting too much. Not everyone's got five daughters to use as work horses like he had."

"How is Elmer these days? I see he's moved into town. He should be in heaven right there on the pond. He can go fishing every day."

"He seems to keep busy with his garden. He's got mostly sand, but with enough rain, he sure grows some fine vegetables and berries. The boys think it's great. They go fishing every time they get near the place. Mabel keeps him in line."

Bill saw the cultivator was finally attached, so they moved out to the shop. "This cultivator attaches in the rear and adjusts to a 36 inch row. The tractor wheels are adjustable for row width also. Loosen these three nuts, set one brake, and the wheel slides right out when you let the clutch out. With most of the other tractors, you have to take the wheel off, and turn it around to make the tires run between the corn rows."

Dad inspected the cultivator with some thoroughness with no comment. Finally he asked, "What will it take to put this in my machine shed? I can see I'd better get the whole package while I'm at it."

"Ed, I want to sell you this tractor. Those boys out there in the valley are going to be buying a tractor one of these days, and I'm sure if I sell you one, some of them will buy one of mine too. I'll give you the best deal in town. I'll throw the cultivator in on the $1,200 plus the old "10-20". How does that sound?"

"It's a start, Bill, but you know you're up against some pretty stiff competition. There were six other tractors demonstrated on the silo filler, and every one of those dealers has the same idea you have. You know I'm going to take advantage of that."

"Give me a chance at the last bid, Ed. That's all I ask."

Finished in town, Dad left for home. Chores were calling. He needed to figure with Mom what they could afford. Dad wasn't a wheeler-dealer, but he was not afraid to put the pressure on in a deal either. They decided the place to start was $600 plus the old tractor. Also, the attached cultivator had to be part of the deal. Horses on a one-row cultivator would not be able to keep up with added corn acreage.

By the middle of September, corn husking and shredding was finished, and the county corn-husking contest was on. Farmers from around the county gathered at one farm to compete with their corn husking skills. It was a festive occasion with a picnic atmosphere. Dad met Earl Peterson, and soon got into tractor talk. The cultivator topic came up, and Earl described his Massy Harris cultivator.

"Ed, our cultivator fits in front of the driver so you see exactly the job you're doing. A support bar goes through the frame just in front of the motor, and the cultivator adjusts on that. Two shovels to cultivate out the rear wheel tracks attach in the rear. The power lift raises and lowers the whole works automatically when you trip the lift lever. The tractor rear wheels need to be turned around to fit between the rows. It takes two to three hours to attach. Let me know next time you're coming up this way, and I can have one put on for you to see."

"I'd like to see that, Earl. I'm sure I'll need that attachment. Old Dick and Dime won't be able to keep pace with the added corn acreage I'll need to put in to pay for a new tractor. Bill Kastner says $1,200 plus the old "10-20" puts his tractor and cultivator in my machine shed today."

"I can beat that by $50," Earl replies without hesitation.

"Sounds like you're in this auction in earnest, Earl. That's good. A little competition can't do me anything but good. I'm going to buy a tractor, and I'd like to get the best deal I can."

"Don't close the deal until you get my final offer, Ed. I need to make some sales out there in the valley to give my products some good exposure. By the way, have there been any reports of deer out in your area? I'm trying to figure out where to go this fall."

"I haven't seen any signs around us. We're planning our usual trip to Eagle River again. I've heard there are quite a few up around Necedah. That's not too far from you."

"I've heard that too. That sounds like a good idea. I might try that. Thanks, Ed."

The festivities took up the day until chore time. Dad felt good. The bidding had started with no commitment on his part.

The next week, miles accumulated on the pick-up truck as Dad drove the seven miles back and forth between Mauston and New Lisbon. The telephone did some of the work, but most of the final bidding was face to face. The price finally came down to $960.00 plus the old "10-20" for the new tractor plus the attached cultivator. Both men offered the same deal. Mom and Dad agreed; it was the best they could do, and the deal was closed.

The Massey Harris was the tractor of choice.

Seven makes of tractor demonstrated on the silo filler in Suldal that year. Over the war years following, five of those tractors ended up in the machine sheds on those farms. Peterson sold two tractors plus additional machinery in the valley, while Kastner sold one tractor, and made enough contacts to sell a number of the "New Idea" products he carried.

The blacksmith converted a lot of horse drawn equipment to use with tractors, and the plowshares wore out even faster keeping him busier than ever. The bank prospered by making several new loans; John even found time to catch a few brook trout in Brewer's Creek

THE WOOD LOT'S HARVEST
A NEW MACHINE SHED

Those Norwegians knew what they were doing when they settled in Suldal Valley. The bottomland was prime for crops, and the wooded bluffs, in addition to reminding them of the "Old" country, provided much needed fuel plus construction material. Now, we've almost forgotten the fuel part; when we do use wood for fuel, it is almost a novelty; a rustic back to nature feeling—a room adornment fireplace.

Any farm without woodland was inferior to one with forested areas. Most farms in the valley had part of their acreage as timber. Now, this might be thought of as unproductive land, but through the mid 1900's, it was a definite necessity. It was usually bluff land, too steep to till and too dense to pasture. It was the source of anything made of wood in addition to many exotic products.

A wood lot had more to offer than just wood for fuel or lumber. Some of those trees were hollow where bees stored their honey. Part of the undergrowth was berry bushes cherished by humans and varmints alike. Some of the varmints were the furry kind. Their pelt in prime brought a welcomed penny. Others were exotic meat on the dinner plate. Sugar maples provided sap to make maple syrup and its by-products. Some forests had such things as chokecherries, crab apples, blackberries or blueberries used for sweets like jams and jellies. Hickory was usually valued for nuts, but the wood also had extra worth. A lone tree in the middle of an open field would usually be a hickory or black walnut, saved during clearing for its bounty of nuts. In most cases that harvest was a matter for the squirrels, but then they had to beware they didn't get harvested for meat.

The most significant harvest was the wood used for the cooking stove. In the winter most farms had a wood-burning furnace. When we became more affluent, we bought coal to stoke the furnace at night.

Summer's harvest was primarily fruit and berries. This was a pleasant chore for Mom and Bob and I. Collecting mushrooms, morels, fruit and berries provided lessons in wild life and nature's ways in addition to the delicacies. Animal behaviors were exposed by unexpected encounters in our search for these hidden treasures.

"Mom! What is that sound? It sounds almost like someone with a drum." Whum--------Whum-----Whum---Whum-Whum Whummmmmmmmm.

"That's a male ruffed grouse beating the air with his wings."

"Why does he do that?"

"He's probably performing for his mate, or maybe he is telling other grouse that this is his territory. Stay away!"

"Mom! What's Whimpy barking at?"

"Lets go see. There he is under that big oak. Can you see anything up there?"

"There's something. It's a squirrel flipping his tail like he's really mad."

"Yes. He's all upset at Whimpy chasing him up a tree and barking at him."

"Those honey bees on the flowers are collecting nectar to take back to their beehive, probably a hollow tree up in the woods someplace. They use the nectar to make honey like we had on our sandwich."

"Can we find the hive?"

"We'll take a cup of sugar and mix it with a cup of water. Then we'll set it out by the flowers and watch to see if a bee comes to drink. When it does, we'll see which way it goes. We'll move the sugar water a ways in that direction and wait until another bee comes. Each time the bee leaves we'll move the dish further in the direction it goes until we get to the honey hive. If the tree is one on our land, we can mark it, and maybe Dad can collect some honey this winter."

The cold season harvest was mainly wood, but it was also the prime season for pelts of most fur bearing varmints. Enterprising individuals often got extra money trapping. Brother Bob had a regular trapping sideline.

Stove-wood and lumber were the major benefits of the woodlot. The Mauer's 120-acre farm was half bluff and creek-bottom. The bluff yielded plenty of wood for the stove. Uncle Art built a circular wood cutting saw to attach to the front of the tractor for cutting logs into stove-wood lengths. The saw swung up over the hood of the tractor for transportation, and was powered by a belt from the tractor.

Oak and pine were the main timber. There were a few hickories usually preserved for their nuts, most of which the squirrels harvested.

When the need for a new machine shed arose, all the lumber came from that woodlot. With a new tractor in the yard and other new equipment likely to follow, it seemed a good idea to build a good machine shed. The old tobacco sheds were getting too dilapidated to use as machine sheds.

Dad met with Lars, the local carpenter, and together they figured out how much, and what kind of lumber was needed. Although he went through only six grades in school, Dad had no problem calculating how many trees to cut to get the required lumber. During August, he marked the trees he would harvest that winter. He wanted to make sure he cut down any dead trees.

The ax was an important tool for winter's work. There were two types, single bit and double bit. The single bit worked as a sledge or hammer as well as an ax. The double bit cut with both sides. I was always impressed by Dad's accuracy with the ax, especially after I had swung it for a while myself. Dad always seemed to hit exactly where he wanted. My efforts seemed to hit anywhere, but where I wanted.

Dad kept his ax sharp at the grindstone. When he swung that ax, wood chips flew, and the timber fell where he wanted it to fall. With the ax, he notched the tree on the side it was to fall. The two-man crosscut saw finished the cut from the other side of the tree. After the tree fell, I helped chop off the branches to be cut up for firewood.

Logs for lumber were piled until a lumber mill came into the neighborhood. Each farmer brought his logs to one farm to be cut into lumber. A good saw man got the most boards with a minimum of waste slabs—pieces with the bark on one side. Slabs weren't wasted. They were used to separate boards while drying, then cut into stove wood.

Dad and George, the hired man, cut wood all winter, and by early spring were ready to haul logs to the saw-mill set up at a neighbor about two miles away. Each tree was cut into the required lengths at the stump. The team dragged the logs to the loading site where they were piled until sawmill time. I helped drag the trimmed branches to another pile to be cut into lengths for the wood burning stove. Some of the oak logs were used for fence posts for fence line repair. Dad split those logs with iron wedges hammered in with the single bit ax or a sledgehammer.

When Dad's turn came at the sawmill, the logs were rolled using a cant hook on to the bobsled bolsters and wrapped with a chain to anchor them to the sled for transport to the mill. Each log was identified with a mark to keep from getting mixed up with the neighbors. At the mill, they rolled each log in turn on to the saw conveyer platform and fixed it in position. Dad told the saw-man what he wanted, and they proceeded to make lumber. George piled the lumber back on the bobsled. Back home they piled it in one of the old tobacco sheds to dry, with some slabs between each layer of boards as spacers so air could freely circulate. Green lumber was not the most desirable.

Construction on the new machine shed started in May. Lars built forms for the cement footings out of lumber, which later would be used as roofing boards. Cement, water, sand and rocks went into the cement mixer. Those rocks were routinely picked up from a hillside field where they seemed to grow. Old wire and some pieces of junk metal, plus the mixed cement went into the forms. After it cured for a week, the forms were removed and construction began.

The building was complete with wood siding, wood shingle roof and sliding doors before threshing started. For a while there was plenty of storage space for things such as extra lumber, bales of hay and supplies besides machinery. That changed as Dad acquired more and more equipment to keep up with the fast moving times.

Many farms leave machinery out in the weather where it rusts away. Dad always coated mole boards, coulters and unpainted metal surfaces with old crank case oil before storage in the shed. When the oil rubbed off next season, the machinery shone like new.

THE FARM WOODLOT

Rural development and urbanization
keep eroding the country woodlot.
Come share with me these memories
that I have almost forgot.

Woodlots were a vital part of farms those days.
Needed fuel and lumber helped pay their way.
Pine, hickory and oak - the trees most plentiful,
These were the lumber of choice, and quite beautiful.
Ax and saw for harvest - simple, cheap and more,
Keeping the wood box full - this child's first chore.
Dad swung his ax - wood chips flew.
Depression worries faded - muscles grew.

That woodland preserve provided
other benefits too,
Relaxation, shelter for animals,
and a picturesque view.
You paid for wild blackberries
with lots of "owie" scratches.
The very best berries hid
in the middle of those patches.

They were generously protected
by thorns that cinched you tight,
Always sharp and wounding
if you tried to fight.

Summer nights, we exercised
"Old Sport" under a full moon.
I can hear it now,
that hound's melodious tune.
His yodeling voice told stories,
hot and cold,
Echoing through those valleys
flooded with moonlight gold.
When he crossed a trail,
it was music to the ear
On wonderful summer nights
so calm and clear.
There were other times
when the nose told the story.
Skunk juice in the face
made him, rolling in the grass, sorry.
"Sport" never could resist
black and white pussy cats.
Every time his fur got wet,
reminded of his latest spats.

Other forest life - birds, beasts,
all kinds of vegetation,
Pique youngster's curiosty -

stimulate imagination.
Strange bird calls—ruffed grouse drumming—
the unique shape of a leaf,
Smells of life decaying,
then renewing beyond belief.
That woodland school taught lessons
children miss these days.
Now these forests are being overrun
by the urban expansion craze.

THAT TRACTOR DRIVING TEEN

One of my passions was driving. It started with the team of horses, but that quickly changed with a taste of gas-powered vehicles.

Equine power became a real drag when the brand new Massey Harris 101 Junior arrived. Then, using the team for just about any job that tractor could do was an abomination, but Dad continued using the horses to do things I felt should be done with gas power. Dad's philosophy was, "Horses get fed whether they work or not; that tractor doesn't eat on idle."

That team had a mind of its own, going where they wanted in spite of my commands. I came to despise working with horses.

I grew into operating the car or tractor gradually, starting with steering the pick-up truck around the farm while sitting on Dad's lap. One thing about farm life; learning to drive was not a competition with road traffic.

I learned stick shifting sitting on the bench seat between Mom and Dad straddling the shift lever; left up – reverse; left down – first; right up – second; right down - 3rd. By the time my legs were long enough to reach the foot pedals,

I knew just about everything required to make the Ford pick-up truck run.

Riding the fender of the old 10-20 McCormick Deering tractor was good training also. I watched how Dad handled each piece of machinery, but it took a man to maneuver that old tractor. With the purchase of the new 101 Junior in 1940, I became a "man," big enough and strong enough to work that tractor by myself. Discing was the perfect starting job. I angled the disc to the operating position, and just drove up and down the field.

Plowing was a challenge. Raising and dropping the plow at the end of the field took timing; too soon left too much headland; too late left some torn up fences. Yank the rope; spin the steering wheel; drive to the next furrow; spin the steering wheel; yank the rope, and follow the furrow to the other end of the field. With keeping track of the plow to see it didn't plug up with stalks, and keeping headed down the furrow; my neck felt like it should be on a swivel.

Then there was the occasional large rock: when the plow hit one of those boulders, it could ruin a plowshare or, worse yet, bend things out of line. The safety-hitch prevented this.

These safety-hitch incidents started with a sudden jerk as the plow hit the rock. This was followed by a jump forward, and a simultaneous raising of my feet to hit the brakes and clutch as the hitch released. The final insult was a slap in the rear as the trip rope broke from the seat where it was tied. It didn't happen too often, but I sure reacted in a hurry when it did.

I loved to cultivate corn. The first time through, shields kept the dirt from covering the small seedlings. Since I tended to speed, this saved a lot of corn. When the corn grew tall and sturdy, the shields were removed from the cultivator so the dirt rolled up to the stalk covering most of the weeds.

When the corn was in check rows, I cultivated both lengthways and crossways. Cultivating crossways was a challenge. Towards the end of the row, the hills of corn never lined up exactly straight. I did a lot of zigzagging back and forth to keep from cultivating out the corn.

The biggest job was attaching the cultivator to the tractor at the beginning of the season, and taking it off at the end. The rear wheels had to be widened. I jacked them off the ground, removed the lug nuts, and turned the wheels around so they ran between the rows. The tire by itself was heavy enough, but these were filled with salt brine for more weight for traction. One fell down once, and I required Dad's help to stand it back up again.

The cultivating season was over when the corn, about knee high, shaded out the row. The weeds didn't grow much in low sunlight. Knee high by the 4th of July meant pretty good corn, and just about the end of the cultivating season.

I never got to use the power take off since all of the machinery was that used with the old 10-20, or converted horse equipment. The major alteration to horse drawn implements was shortening the tongue for attachment to the tractor draw bar. I rejoiced when the tongue was shortened on the manure spreader, mower and hay wagon. We'd never use them with the horses again.

Like most teenagers, I tried to make things go fast or faster. The motor on the new tractor ran at 1500 RPMs at full throttle; except in 4th (road gear) where full throttle was another three notches and 1800 RPMs. A little lever on the governor controlled the RPMs. It didn't take long before I figured out how to run at 1800 RPMs in all gears. I shifted to 4th, pulled the throttle wide open, then back to the desired gear and away I went. Dad probably knew what was going on, but never said anything. The disc really threw the dirt as that tractor zipped across the field.

It was a real challenge to back up a four-wheel wagon behind the tractor. Things don't always go in the anticipated direction. It was almost like a chess game. It was complicated.

I was thrilled one day when Dad let me back the thresher up to the barn at a neighbor's farm. It was easier than usual though since, for this alignment, the thresher was attached to the front-end hitch on the tractor taking away the rear view mirror effect. I pushed those four wheels right where I wanted like I'd been doing it all my life. Pushing four wheels was a lot easier than backing them. I also lined the tractor up for the drive belt. When tractor and thresher were not lined up properly, the belt ran off the pulley. Just moving the front end of the tractor slightly left or right made the belt move away from or back to the center of the pulley.

Most tractors have separate brakes for the rear wheels. This originally was to shift power to the non-slipping wheel. The brakes could also assist in steering. Hitting the left brake forced the front of the tractor to the left and visa versa. This was especially effective with Farmall-type front wheels (the tricycle arrangement). I quickly mastered this maneuver, using the brakes to dodge the corn seedlings when cultivating crossways.

It was fashionable to have a spinner knob on the steering wheel, since power or hydraulic steering was unheard of. I got one and put it in place soon after I started driving the tractor. That worked fine except when some interruption to the line of travel caused the tractor to turn. Then, if I wasn't gripping the steering wheel tight, that knob whacked my thumb as that wheel spun. With a change in the weather, that thumb still feels the effects of that out of control steering knob.

Modern day tractors still resemble the old, but with all the electronics, hydraulics, power controls, and even satellite monitors; I would have to go back to school to learn how to operate one.

TRACTOR DRIVING THERAPY

Driving my John Deer tractor
makes me feel like a kid again.
It brings back all those memories
of sunshine and rain.

"Buster, when you can,
use the team instead.
Those horses on idle
still have to be fed."
Dad's philosophy
surely made sense,
But for this tractor driving teen,
he was just being dense.

Kick the lift, hit one brake,
spin the steering wheel;
Drop the plow, pull the throttle,
we're in business with steel.
If I did it just right,
it was like a symphony.
If I did it out of step,
the end of the row's in jeopardy.

Then there was the fence,
it got torn out once or twice
When the tractor got too close
and the maneuver wasn't nice.
It was my favorite toy,
that tractor, brand new.
It could do most anything
that kid asked it to.

Now --- just one pass with the rototiller
and I'm ready to plant grain.
Still --- driving my John Deer tractor
makes me feel like that kid again.

THE THRESHING CREW REWARD

Mom had little time for cooking fancy cakes and pies. Her specialty was meat and potatoes with vegetables from the garden. By 1940, I had heard lots of stories about the great feasts served the threshers. As an eleven-year-old, I loved dessert. How could I join the crew, and enjoy those mouth-watering meals?

One or two men from each neighboring farm made up the crew. That was ten to twelve men the women fed at each noon meal. To prepare for and serve this many men, the women helped each other. Each cook took pride in her own specialty. During the war years, some hoarded their sugar ration stamps just to be able to serve their famous desserts to the threshing crew.

Grasses like oats, wheat, barley and rice grow their mass of seeds in individual husks at the end of a stem. When the dry stem with its seeds is flailed against something hard, it separates into seeds and straw. The straw is light and the seeds are relatively heavy so they easily separate with a wind. The threshing machine (in some places called a separator) does this separating job.

Oat threshing happened between late July and early August. Dad pulled the thresher out of storage with the tractor, and backed it up to the barn. He greased all the bearings, installed the belts, and was ready for the first wagonload of bundles from the field by 10 AM.

Tim handled the bagger. I started to help him hoist the full bags of oats on to the grain wagon. It wasn't long before Tim showed me how to tie the bags shut with a special knot, and how to put a new bag on the grain delivery spout.

When the thresher moved to the next farm, Tim asked me to come along and help him. Great! I was a member of the crew. Now I'd find out if the stories about the meals were really true.

Helping Tim bag the oats was my first threshing crew job. As I matured, I advanced to other tasks but bagging, giving me rights to dinner, was the first and most rewarding job.

Those threshing crew meals, especially desserts, were everything I had dreamed they would be.

THE THRESHING CREW LUNCH

Lunchtime for the threshing crew
was something to behold.
That meal contrived by the different cooks
was revered in stories told.
You'd better bring your appetite,
it would be satisfied, that's true.
No appetizer needed here,
hunger grew working on that crew.
Capacities were famous,
each man left with his belly full.
The stories told, oft repeated,
mostly a lot of bull.
Chicken and dumplings, pork roast well done,
maybe a beef stew.
Potatoes and gravy, all kinds of vegetables
straight from the garden to you.
Pies and puddings, custards and meringue;
better not be late.
Thinking of those wonderful desserts
makes the mouth salivate.
Lemonade to wash it down,

always real home-made.
No wonder they have their siestas
lying in the shade.

Now I think about it time and again,
eating frozen chicken pot pie,
Warmed in that "have to have" microwave
without which I would die.
My muscles grew on that crew,
with all that exercise.
That wonderful time has come and gone,
I still think of it with sighs.

THE 4-H CLUB PROJECT

The 4-H club is designed for country kids to encourage interest in and growth of their farm skills. They learn to produce a product to show at the county fair in competition with other kids. Projects include: sewing, baking, vegetable gardens, calves, hogs, sheep, chickens; most anything connected with farming.

In 1939, Mom and Dad convinced me to have a calf for my 4-H club project. Dad said I could have Flower's calf if it was a heifer.

One sunny morning in August, Flower, the best milking Guernsey in the barn, didn't come in with the rest of the cows. Dad knew she had her calf in the pasture. After he finished milking we drove the pick-up truck down to the creek. Flower was across the stream standing nearby some tall grass at the edge of an alder thicket. Dad waded across. As he got close to the tall grass, the calf jumped up to run. He caught it easily, and carried it back to the truck. I restrained the calf in the back of the truck as we drove slowly back to the barn. Flower followed close behind, bawling to her baby. It was a nice heifer, and with a mother called Flower, her name had to be Blossom. Since she was born before the first of the year, she was classed as a senior as opposed to a junior heifer.

Blossom suckled milk from her mother for two days to get the all-important colostrum vital for her health. She had to drink milk from a pail after that. Teaching her to drink was a lesson in behavior for both Blossom and me.

The instinct to nurse is very strong. Calves in a pen together often suck each other's ears so it's not hard to get them to suck a finger. The calf's instinct is to reach up to the udder to nurse instead of down into a pail of milk. It takes patience to teach a calf to drink from a bucket.

I got into the pen with two-day old Blossom and a calf pail with a little milk in it. I had no trouble getting her to suck my fingers, but she wanted to reach up as normal with nursing. Finally I got her muzzle down a little ways into the pail but not far enough to reach the milk. More milk would work so I filled the bucket half full. Now Blossom was so anxious she butted the pail, and spilled half the milk. That was frustrating. I refilled with more milk and with four fingers in her mouth, led her nose down into the bucket. As she sucked she started to get some milk. Gradually, I withdrew my fingers. She kept on sucking for several seconds before withdrawing her muzzle. My hand went back into her mouth, and she followed it back down again. A few more times, and she had all the milk she needed. In the morning things were much easier. By evening, all she needed was starting, and she finished on her own. She was bucket trained. I claimed Blossom for my 4-H club calf to show at the fair.

Blossom shared a box stall with another calf her age. The manger always had some good quality hay in it, and twice a day I gave them a little ground corn and oats. By the time they were weaned they ate hay and grain, and were chewing their cud like ruminants should.

Training Blossom to lead with a halter was a challenge. I was a born procrastinator. By the time I started training her, she weighed more than I did. Lessons started as a pulling contest. Blossom with four feet had more traction than I did. I soon learned to use my head or she would lead me. Get the halter on and leave it tied to something solid until she learned when the rope was tight she wasn't going anywhere. That was fine in the calf pen, but outside she could run and did. I stuck with her, got her head turned, and finally stopped.

It wasn't long before she began to obey the halter, and enjoyed going out for showing lessons. She liked a little run to start each lesson, but soon learned to obey her halter commands.

The finish of the 4-H project was showing in competition at the county fair. Blossom competed as a senior open class Guernsey. All the club calves were housed in the same building so kids observed different ways to prepare their calves for showing. Some beef animals were clipped in a special way to make their shape more ideally proportioned. Milking cows were left with some quarters partially filled to give the udder a more desirable balanced shape. This didn't make an impression at the time, but later it seemed a bit deceitful.

There were lots of 4-H kids with their calves. They all brushed, curried, shined and polished their animals each day getting them ready for judging. On judging day everyone dressed in his or her clean cloths. I gave Blossom extra care. Her tail was all bushed out like a fancy hair-do. I led her around so she got rid of some of her energy before the show. I didn't want her leading me around the ring.

All the calves were led in a circle around the judge. Each time they stopped, I made Blossom stand in a pose designed to make her look her best. Finally the judge lined us up with the winner at the head. Blossom took third place with a white ribbon in a class of ten. After I took her back to the calf stalls, my mind turned to entertainment—the carnival rides and more exhibits.

On the last day of the fair, all the 4-H calves joined with the rest of the livestock in the parade past the grandstand. One girl had a very embarrassing time. Her yearling heifer was in heat. While the heifer behaved perfectly well normally, in the parade she just wouldn't do anything right. She wanted to run, and then she got stubborn and wouldn't move. That poor girl couldn't get through with the parade fast enough. Blossom saw the other heifer dancing around, and tried a little dancing herself, but I kept her under control getting through the parade in good shape.

After the fair we put Blossom out to pasture with the rest of the heifers, and I went back to driving the tractor whenever I had the chance.

By fifteen months of age, Blossom was well past puberty. One day when she was in heat, I lead her to the neighbor's to be bred. She had a bull calf in nine months. Now a cow, she became a member of the milking herd, and took her place with the rest of the cows. She didn't take long to learn which stanchion was hers. I put her in an empty stanchion the first day after she calved. After that, if she got into the wrong space, the cow that usually stood in that spot rooted her out. She soon learned which was her place.

Now the dairying side of the business began. I sat down on my milk stool on her right side. Her udder was swollen and hard so I tried to rub out the swelling. She kicked a bit but the rubbing soothed her. Slowly squeezing a teat while my head was against her flank, I could feel her tense to kick. I grabbed her left leg with my left hand above the knee blocking the kick. She tried a couple more times as I squeezed the teats, but finally relaxed and let me finish. The colostrum milk her calf didn't drink, I collected the first two days after calving, and fed to the hogs. After that, all the milk went into the separator, and Blossom enjoyed life as the newest member of the milking herd competing with Flower for herd milking honors, earning her keep.

PISCATORIAL BEGINNINGS

Brewer's creek originated from springs in the bluffs around Suldal Valley. It was barely visible in the tall grass until a large spring just above the "holes"—a stretch where the water ran under ground—almost doubled the volume making the stream too wide to jump across without getting wet. It ran through the farm Bob and I grew up on, winding its way some five miles to the Lemonweir River. It was icy cold, rarely if ever freezing in the winter, perfect brook trout territory. Alder brush, thick along parts of the stream was always available to use as a country boy's fishing pole. I could just break off a long straight piece of brush, strip off the branches, tie the line to the end, and I was ready to go fishing.

Bob's birthday was the 15th of May, the opening day of fishing season in Wisconsin in the thirties and forties. We celebrated it every year by skipping school to go fishing. With a trout stream running through the farm and Mother taking her two sons fishing as toddlers, it's no wonder, we both grew up loving fishing. A couple years of Mother's tutoring at the "holes," and that stream was heaven to us boys.

The flood plain along the stream was quite swampy. It never became an engineering project for straightening or attempted cultivation. The closest that stream came to farming was as a watering hole for cattle.

Our cows drank from a wide spot in the stream. That wide spot also served as the swimming hole. It was only deep enough to get our rear ends wet if we lay down. Junior, our next-door neighbor, went swimming with Bob and I one unusually warm 21st of March. That put us on his mother's bad boys list. Junior could have caught a cold because of us.

The stream wandered its way between alder brush and an occasional elm, oak or weeping willow some five miles to the river. There was a potential spot for trout to hide on every washed out bend. Watercress along much of the shore line strangled the stream into a fast flowing current challenging a fisherman's ability to get his baited hook down deep enough so the fish saw it before it passed them. As the stream wandered towards town it got wider and deeper - never much more than a little over the knees except under a couple of bridges where roads crossed.

Spring rains and cloudbursts occasionally flooded the stream with muddy water overflowing the banks into nature's natural shock absorbers, the swamps. Here, the silt settled, and clear water slowly seeped back into the brook. Muddy water was tough to fish in, but as it cleared, we fished it whenever we had the chance.

A big squirming angleworm or night crawler was the bait of choice, but late in the season grasshoppers were also popular bait. When the ground got dry, worms were harder to find. Grasshoppers made a faster get-away possible before Dad caught us if a shower halted haying. Moving up or down the stream, we caught the grasshoppers as we used them.

The second stimulus to our fishing penchant was a one-week fishing trip every year. Sometime between corn planting and haying, we reserved a week for vacation. Uncle Tom's cabin (no relation) on a bay in the Wisconsin River just out of Tomahawk was the favored spot. Bob and I fished off a little wooden bridge stretching to a small wooded island. In the evening with a worm and a bamboo cane pole, we caught some of the biggest bullheads we'd ever seen. They didn't have to be very big to beat anything we caught in Brewer's creek. One day, I went over to the little island and saw the biggest snake I had ever seen. I was leery of going over there alone after that. Our first experience with bluegills also came on these trips.

Uncle Art, in his spare time fashioned a mobile camper by building a small house on the back of a Model T Ford truck. We used it once on a fishing trip to Gull Lake in northern Wisconsin.

The Model T didn't have enough power to get up a very steep hill on the way to the lake. This problem was solved by putting blocks behind the rear wheels, then revving the motor and letting the clutch out fast. The truck lurched ahead a few feet before it stalled, and the blocks were set behind the wheels again. Then the whole process started over. We made it up the hill without burning up the clutch. With that new camper on a sandy beach, and a well point driven in the beach for fresh water, we had all the comforts of home.

In 1932 while things were being loaded at my grandparent's farm for the trip, I was left with a teenage aunt at the home farm. I was getting awfully anxious so Aunt Cassie devised a way to keep me occupied. She found some game to play telling me as soon as we started playing the game the car would come. Sure enough, we just got started, and here came the car around the bluff. I sure thought that aunt was smart.

In the mid thirties, my grandparents retired from their farm, and moved to town. Their new home was right on a flowage of the Lemonweir River. Bob and I occasionally stayed overnight with Grandma and Grandpa. Fishing was the objective whenever someone could be enticed to take out the rowboat. Trolling for crappies in the evenings was always a great thrill.

I saw or heard this somewhere. It fits our philosophy just right, " *A bad day fishing is better than a good day doing anything else.*" Every moment spent fishing added more happy hours to our lives.

FISHING BROTHERS

The memories are fine, brother of mine,
of days we spent fishing together,
For northern and bass along shore near the grass,
in any and all kinds of weather.
I'd run the oars, maneuvering the shores,
you'd cast to your spot, I to mine.
It was always a job getting back to the dock,
we never made it on time.
We learned all there was piscatorially
while making our rowing muscles sore
And when we got that outboard motor
we could fish a whole lot more.

That cloud, we'd pray, could stop and delay
haying until tomorrow.
Escape to the creek again this week
never was a sorrow.
We knew every curve and snag on that stream
where a trout might be hiding and more,
Walking around without making a sound,
improved our chances to score.

We met more than one envious fisherman,
    carrying fancy rod and reel,
Who wondered how we got all those trout
    while they couldn't get one feel.

Those were the days reveries crave
    to go back to now and again.
We in our memories do that quite easily
    without any noticeable strain.

THE ONE-ROOM COUNTRY SCHOOL

It was classed as a one-room schoolhouse,
really it had more.
The hall in front, a small kitchenette
and the woodshed in the back made four,
Hats and coats hung in the hallway
plus the rope to ring the school bell.
Wood and that freestanding furnace
warmed that room quite well.
The kitchenette was an addition
when the school lunch program began.
Add two outhouses at the back;
to them in the winter kids ran.
Miss Benson, the single schoolteacher
was of local Norwegian extraction.
She performed that job efficiently
with admirable perfection.

Teaching is a major challenge for anyone especially in a one-room school. Enrollment in the Suldal School was twenty to thirty kids, grades one thru eight. The subjects taught were the three R's, plus music, acting and art.

The room was arranged with large blackboards across the front faced by a row of chairs for the students. The teacher had her desk in one corner at the front facing the student desks. Each class moved at the prescribed time to the chairs in front of the blackboard to recite their lessons.

The younger students sat in the small desks on one side of the room and the older students, sat in the larger desks toward the other side. All the desks faced the front of the room.

I had the same teacher for the first six grades. She made class work enjoyable, but recess was always the favored part of the day. Swings and teeter-totters occupied one side of the schoolyard, and field games (soft ball and football) the other. When snow was on the ground, snowball fights, all kinds of games and of course sledding used up most of the energy.

A steep bluff right across the road provided the slope for sledding. All the kids brought their sleds, and at recess, raced up that trail along the woods to a starting point way up by the rock face. I always went as high as I could go. With a running flying leap I shot down that hill like a rocket. A good run carried across the road, clear past the schoolhouse. From one direction, traffic wasn't visible until the sled was in the middle of the road. Horse and bobsled was about all the traffic there was. I never worried about a car.

My cousins had a pair of skis, and made a little ski jump half way down the steep part of the slope. Since the jump was made of snow, steel runners cut it up pretty fast so no one was supposed to sled over it. I went over it at least once. Things like that broke all the boards in my sled, and spread the runners so its belly dragged.

For Christmas that year Dad took the sled to Uncle Art's blacksmith shop, welded some iron in an arc from runner to runner to keep them from splaying out again, and replaced all the broken wood with oak boards. I thought that was the greatest Christmas present I ever got. Within a week, I had one of the bed boards broken off behind the last cross brace, probably from going off that jump one more time.

One year the school had a practice teacher, Robert White, for a few weeks in the fall. He had played football in high school in New Lisbon. At recess everyone played football. I, as the biggest kid in school, had to be on the opposite team to the teacher. I blocked into him as hard as I could every play until one time, just as we hit, he flipped his hip out towards me. I thought I ran into a stone wall. I never did that again (without pads on anyhow).

At school I was just another first grader among all the upper classes. I learned to get along with the other kids. I seemed to be bigger than my classmates but avoided fights. The only way they could get to me was teasing about girls. I hated that. That one room schoolhouse educated me in more than the 3 R's.

I had an older cousin who walked cross-country nearly two miles to school. He caught the road close to our house so we walked together. That made the introduction to school less stressful. The walk to school was an education in itself; observing wild life, throwing rocks at telephone insulators, sticking my tongue on the cold metal bridge rail, and throwing snowballs. Nature's ebb and flow was a continuing story. It challenged the mind to understand how and why things work. I never was bored with nature's teachings. That one room school taught me the tools and knowledge to make my way in this life, but nature's beauty and diversity observed on the way to and from school also significantly influenced my perspective.

Buster started in the first grade seats
sitting quiet as a mouse.
Learned his alphabet from A to Z,
in that one room country schoolhouse,
Watched the blackboard in the front,
listened in on lessons of all grades.
Heard the stories over and over
of Dick and Jane's dull escapades.
He tried to read classic novels,
they didn't capture his attention.
In grade 5 was doing grade 7 and 8
division and multiplication.
He could see with his new eyeglasses,
the blackboard no longer in a haze.
Lenses got broken more than once,
he rough-housed a bit those days.
He penciled pages on pages of spirals,
practicing perfect O's.

Didn't help his penmanship a bit,
could hardly read his own prose.
He never was that ardent
for academics or sporting competition.
Things came too easy for that kid,
he had to marry to get ambition.

YOU NEVER HAD IT SO GOOD

Farm life has a reputation of being dismal and dull, nothing but work and drudgery with meager returns. Let me tell you how I remember it. My first twelve years span the entire "Great Depression".

There wasn't much money spent on frivolous things such as entertainment. The daily newspaper had comic strips. I read them eagerly. The family radio insured up to the minute news and there were programs to entertain any age group. Cowboy stories and mysteries captured my imagination. As soon as the mail arrived, I collected it, flopped in front of the radio, and opened to the comic strips. Propped on two elbows, I read while listening to the radio. In the evening, Rossini's "William Tell Overture" announced the start of my favorite program, "The Lone Ranger". On Saturday night the whole family listened to Lulu Belle and Scottie with the WLS "Barn Dance". Whenever Joe Lewis had a boxing match, Dad tried to get chores done early. More times than not he missed the match due to an early knockout. That's about the only thing Dad had against Lewis. There was rarely time or money for a movie, but when there was, Gene Autry and Roy Rogers were the favorites. Dad enjoyed Gene's singing.

There never was a lack of things to do, and money was of little use to me. There were no drug stores for ice cream or candy on the farm. As I paged through the "Montgomery Ward" and "Sears Roebuck" catalogues, such things as a Red Ryder BB gun or fancy sled were tempting, but these were the carrots to entice me into some new job.

Playtime was spontaneous; use what you have and whatever works. "Cowboys and Indians" was a favorite game. Broken corncobs were ammunition. They rarely put out a window. They were too light. They didn't hurt when you hit someone either. I never knew there was such a thing as a "Depression". As far as I was concerned this was "The Way It Was".

Hollyhocks grew around the porch: prolific, self-seeding, pastel-colored, wide mouthed flowers. The seeds were unique; small discs stacked side by side in a circle around the core of a pod like a miniature tire. They were easy to harvest when dried. I collected them one year but lost interest by next years planting season. That was probably fortunate. There'd have been hollyhocks all over the place.

Dress code was bib-overalls. I was a fast growing boy, suspenders allowed me to wear clothes longer by adjusting the shoulder straps. Somewhere in my pre-teens I became clothes conscious enough to notice other kids wore pants with a belt. I really felt in style when I finally got pants with a belt.

Another cloths must was hi-top leather boots. Those shoes in the catalogue looked like my style, just right for a hunter. When I finally got a pair, I soon tired of them. It took so long to lace them up, and then barefoot season came along where I just slipped on my pants, and was ready to go. By the next cold season loafers were in style.

A job for any age was easy to find on the farm. My first regular job was keeping the wood box filled. All the cooking was done on that stove so the wood box had to be kept full. This job introduced me to responsibility. If the wood box was empty someone else had to fill it, and was sure to let me know about it.

Mother split wood for the stove. When a chunk wouldn't stand up properly, she propped it up against another chunk and held it at the bottom with one foot. One day with an extra effort swing the ax went clear through the chunk, her shoe and her little toe. With a bandage wrapped around the toe it healed leaving a scar. I always worried about my foot holding a chunk in place when I was splitting wood after that.

Robert Frost's Grindstone poem was almost an exact picture of my experience with the grindstone. Dad did a lot of work with the ax and always kept it sharp. The ax and the scythe both were sharpened on the grindstone. I provided some of the turning power for that honing wheel.

The wood-burning stove provided heat, humidity and a cooking surface. That stove radiated heat throughout the kitchen and living room. When we came in cold from playing in the snow, we sat on the oven door and toasted. It wasn't long before we were dry and warm and ready to go again.

Gathering eggs from the hen house was another early job. I picked up the eggs every afternoon. This was a more responsible job. Eggs were fragile and easily cracked.

Kids knew where Dad and Mom worked. They were out there with them every day, even helped them sometimes. When helping became an assigned job, appreciation grew. It didn't take long before Dad and Mom went through the valley of being awfully dumb, and back to the pedestal of being pretty darn smart.

Farm life was filled with many dangers ranging from being kicked, butted, scratched or bit by animals, to being grabbed or run over by mechanical monsters, all with unforgiving tempers. I learned to approach animals carefully. Surprising a horse, pig or cow resulted in unexpected behavior; a kick, stampede or bite. I learned to respect both ends of the animal. The swinging head could be as painful as a kicking foot and the flailing tail, while not lethal, was more than disturbing, especially if it had been soaking in the gutter. The mechanical monsters gave me a few bumps and bruises; just enough to make me realize they played for keeps.

Trips to town were real Saturday adventures, especially in winter when the snow was too deep for the car. Dick and Dime pulling the bobsled was transportation to town on those days. The sled was filled with soft straw. We were bundled in our warmest clothes, and burrowed in that straw, we had a wonderful time.

The main stop in town was Uncle Art's blacksmith shop where we played with cousins, and watched the mighty smithy work his wonders. That forge heating up a plowshare interested me. The bellows blew air through the coals until the plowshare buried in them glowed white-hot. It was ready to be shaped, sharpened and tempered. I watched the metal being hammered into shape on the anvil so it had the right draw to turn the soil properly. It was mystifying. Just dipping the hot piece of metal into that barrel of water made it hard as steel. It was all a wonder.

The planer amazed me. The rough sawmill board went into the machine, and came out the other end, finished smooth as glass. Our cousins and Bob and I rolled and played in the shavings which were also used as bedding for our baby chicks.

The arc welder was scary. I was warned not to look at it while Uncle Art was welding. Sparks flew and it made a crackling noise that didn't invite confidence about its safety. I could look at those flying sparks through a mask with special glass, but all I could see then was the sparks and nothing else. Time to go home always came too soon.

A farm family was not complete without a dog. Whimpy was ours. He was a small dog of mixed breeding: terrier face, collie coloring, medium length hair, one of the gang. He went everywhere with us. He was a good hunting dog, hunted anything: squirrels, rabbits, pheasants, he even seemed to know when I was hunting sparrows. When Whimpy saw anyone with the gun, he got all excited. "Are we going down to the creek or up to the bluff?" When hunting pheasants in swamp grass, we knew he was getting close to a bird when he started springing in the air to see it. Get ready. That pheasant was about to explode out of its cover.

I often cut across the creek on a short cut to school. I noticed a bunch of the fence posts had woodpecker holes in them. Each of those holes had a bluebird nest in it. A week or so later almost all the baby bluebirds had died and were just rotting in the nests. I never did find an explanation as to what happened, and also never saw them nesting there again.

Walking by the creek one day, I spied a trail through the swamp grass. The grass was flattened into the water making a path almost a foot wide. The trail led to a big snapping turtle who, when he noticed me, buried himself in the mud. I tried but couldn't get him out of the mud. Later, I saw another trail. This time, I captured the turtle by getting a stick under it before it got buried in the mud. Some people paid good money for a big turtle like that for soup. I played with it a while, but soon tired and let it go.

Nature was always challenging with lots of questions and also a few answers.

The most important chore with dairy cattle was milking since that brought in the money. That became a regular job for me when I was about 10 years old. The inducement was a new bicycle. Initially, the milking was all by hand. It didn't hurt me a bit. I was always noted for a strong grip, which I attributed to squeezing those teats twice a day. It was a monotonous job, sitting, automatically squeezing those teats. Swallows nests right over my head entertained me most of the summer. At other times there always seemed to be something to watch or think about while milking.

The bicycle was a constant companion. It went everywhere with me, from the creek bottoms to the bluffs. The only thing it didn't do was follow along as I walked. I always had to go back and pick it up when finished fishing or hunting. The mechanic in me profited from that bike. The sandy roads meant sand got in the bearings so there was reason to take the wheels off to clean or replace a bearing. Rinsing the bearing in gasoline got rid of the sand. It seemed worth it when I realized how much better the bike ran after proper maintenance. It would coast for miles after a good cleaning.

All the bluffs and creek bottoms meant Suldal Valley had plenty of places for winter sports; all the way from skiing, sledding and tobogganing on the slopes to building igloos and carving caves out of snow drifts to ice skating on frozen ponds or ice rinks in town.

Sunday afternoon was the time for kids to get together. If it was for tobogganing, one family had a big toboggan, and a clear slope to slide on. The top of the hill didn't seem too high until about half way up. Dragging that toboggan got pretty tedious. At the top, arranging the seating order, boy, girl, boy, girl, boy, could be significant. Who got to sit behind whom was meaningful. When everyone was finally seated and we pushed off, WOW! That two-minute ride almost made up for the twenty-minute drag back up the hill. About three rides and it was time for something else, maybe sitting in front of the fire to get dried out.

Sledding was an individual challenge, how high could you go, how fast could you go and how far could you go? Some sleds just seemed to do a better job than others. Most of the slopes had too many obstacles to steer around for kids to use uncontrollable inner tubes or corrugated box sleds.

One winter Sunday, the cousins with the skis and some other kids in the community were at our house. We all went up to the bluff to do some sledding and skiing. I went to the top of the twisting bluff road, stepped into the straps on the cousin's skis, and started down the trail. I knew nothing about snowplow turns or any other kind of maneuvering, but I negotiated the first switchback successfully. By the second turn, I was going faster. Sailing sideways into that tree trunk, I should have broken both legs. Thanks to a diet with plenty of milk in it, all I got was a healthy respect for skiers. I didn't try that again until an army buddy, formerly with the college ski patrol, showed me how to fall and turn.

Ice-skating was learning how to stay on my feet. It was good advice not to skate too close to me. Although I rarely fell, my flailing arms and legs made me a hazard. Tag with safety zones only occupied by the last person in the center circle was the main game. Hockey was any old stick, and a tin can for a puck.

The energy used in these games was tremendous. I usually was wetter on the inside from sweat than on the outside from snow. There was the occasional accident, but usually just bruised pride.

By the time school ended for the summer, Bob and I were going barefoot all day. We loved it. Mother said, "Boys, don't take your shoes off until the first whip-poor-will arrives in the spring." We never lasted that long. We went to school barefoot. Mother even had trouble getting shoes on us for church. Tom and Huck had nothing on the two of us. Our feet were so callused we never noticed things, which now would bring a shout of pain. When the roads were first graveled, it was so nice for driving, but when walked on with bare feet, it was a curse.

The depression child complained of things he didn't have, just as kids do these days. The memories of those good old days are enchanting. We lived intimate with nature, and learned its lessons in spite of ourselves. Its message helped shape our lives, in different ways. The looking back view is unique to each of us.

These days, most kids, "Never had it so good."

CHICKENS ON THE FARM

"Where's Buster?" was Mom's most common query when this five year old was missing from the house.

One afternoon she thought, "The mailman delivered two hundred day-old leghorn pullets yesterday in four cardboard boxes with breathing holes in the top. I bet he's out there in the brooder house watching those chicks running around on the shavings his dad brought back from town. He can't figure how they can take care of themselves with no mom."

During the depression of the thirties, chickens were a substantial provider for many farmers. The operation size ranged from a few hens and a rooster roaming the yard providing eggs and meat for home use, to a few hundred hens in a confining hen house producing eggs and meat to sell for cash.

Most farms in Suldal Valley were diversified dairy farms. Dairy was the main source of income: but hogs, poultry and occasional cash crops, such as tobacco, potatoes or sweet corn, supplemented the cash flow.

Poultry converted green grass, insects, animal matter and grains into a useful end product—eggs and meat.

Gathering the eggs every day was one of the earliest jobs for children on the farm. If the eggs were left in a nest for too long, they could spoil. Furthermore, if a hen found her nest full of eggs, she would begin to "set," and stop laying. The surplus of eggs—what exceeded home use—brought real money, so that when children became egg custodians, they experienced the rewards of responsibility. If they broke an egg, they were throwing away money.

On farms where poultry was a significant source of income, day-old- chicks were purchased in late winter from a hatchery. We bought Leghorns, a breed strictly for egg production.

The chick's first home was the brooder house, a small building, usually on skids so it could be pulled to different locations. The chicks were let outside to scavenge and exercise as they matured and the weather warmed.

The brooder house had a source of heat. In the early thirties, an oil or kerosene space heater warmed the whole building. By the mid thirties, the heater was replaced by an electric incubator, a four to five foot square low pyramid-shaped hood with the outer edges five to six inches off the floor. A canvas skirt was attached around the edge reaching to the floor except for scallops, about every six inches, where the chicks could run in and out. A low wattage light bulb and a thermostatically controlled heat element kept the temperature under the hood comparable to that under a mother hen.

Chickens provided an animal behavior lesson for me. When the baby chicks arrived, I sat for hours in that brooder house watching them run out from under that hood to eat and drink, and back under to get warm. I was curious about how those chicks knew enough to take care of themselves without a mother.

One chick sometimes pecked another chick until it got a bleeding sore. That was fatal, because the rest of the chicks then pecked at that bleeding spot. They were regular cannibals. Replacing the white light bulbs with red ones reduced this problem. The chicks couldn't tell what was blood and what wasn't.

As the down was replaced by feathers and the chicks grew too large for the incubator; they were let outside to supplement their diet with grass, insects and whatever else they could find. When the pullets began laying eggs, they were moved to the main hen house. It had nest boxes, roosts and feeders with special feed to stimulate egg production. At first pullets produce small eggs. As they mature, eggs are larger and marketable.

One year Dad moved the brooder house to a hay field just after it was cut and put up in cocks. The pullets were big enough to be let out so the brooder house door was left open all night. The chickens would go out as soon as it was daylight. After the morning milking, Dad discovered a bunch of dead pullets around the brooder house, some stuffed under haycocks.

A fox with a den of cubs up on the bluff must have seen those chickens. This was her opportunity for an easy meal. She came down at daylight when no one was around and made a cache to use later on. Dad built a blind on top of the brooder house, and got up before daylight to surprise the old vixen, but she was too elusive to hit with the rifle. Therefore, the pullets had to be locked up at night, and let out after everyone was up in the morning. The fox wouldn't risk coming down off the bluff out into the open hay field in broad daylight.

Chicks have an instinctive fear of flying predators. When they saw a hawk or crow fly over, no matter how high, one chick gave a little 'eek' and everyone ran for cover.

Rats overpopulated one year. They found a hole in a corner of the hen house, and came in after the chickens went to roost at night. Whimpy learned if he went in with us after dark, rats would be there. He was right at the door as it opened, and streaked immediately to the corner the rats came in. The rats ran too but Whimpy got there before they all got out. He grabbed one and shook it until it was dead and then another. He eliminated a lot of rats at that hole. He was a great rat destroyer.

Another money crop with chickens was raising them for meat. One year Mother bought a bunch of Rhode Island Red chicks, a meat breed, and used the extra skim milk mixed with ground corn to fatten them. When fattened they were shipped to market as a cash crop. That lasted one year so it must not have been too profitable.

Feathers were prized by a lot of nesting birds. After the chicken house manure was spread on a field, sparrows, starlings, swallows and other birds soon picked up the small feathers for lining their nests. Nothing went to waste.

Nature's system provided a constant school for the inquisitive mind. Whether they knew it or not, youngsters on the farm got an early and continual lesson in Biology.

ENGLISH SPARROWS

Mother bought a "Birds of America" book for the family. Keeping track of the time of arrival of different birds in the spring and entering the dates in that book encouraged our interest in wildlife and nature. I learned to identify most of the native species by looking at the beautiful pictures and reading about them.

English sparrows found farms very inviting. There was plenty of food to eat and lots of places to build nests. As a result they over populated and became pests. These sparrows made a terrible mess with their nests and waste. They were also quite aggressive and drove away less dominant species such as blue birds and cliff swallows. They used blue bird's nest sites and appropriated cliff swallow's nests for themselves.

I hated these bullies and did my best to discourage them around the farm. My first kill with my Red Ryder BB gun was an English sparrow. I tried to drive them away by pulling down their nests whenever and wherever possible.

The old tobacco shed was a favorite sparrow-nesting place. They built nests in almost every corner where a rafter met the side of the shed. The shed was not used for tobacco anymore, but the poles where tobacco had been hung were still there. I climbed up the inside of the shed, and walked across on those poles to reach most of the nests. I periodically pulled them out. The nests were made of dried grass, hay and straw to form an enclosure with feathers as the lining. The sparrows just picked up the pieces, jammed them back in the corners and laid another batch of eggs.

One day I was walking across on a pole at the highest level. As I got to the middle of the pole it slipped off its support on one end. I hit the dirt floor hard and ran to the house bawling with dirty pants—dirty on the inside as well as outside. I learned to look at the ends of those poles to see that they were well on their support after I fell one more time from a lower level.

Another favored nesting site was the cupola in the center of the barn roof. I shinnied from the end to the center of the barn on the hayfork track to get to the cupola. That track was in the peak of the roof, fifteen to twenty feet off the floor. The sparrows nested in spring and early summer when the hayloft was almost empty. I traversed that track at least two times. The sparrow and pigeon nests all hit the floor. Those pigeon nests placed on a wide ledge were a real mess. Those baby pigeons just backed up to the edge of the nest to go to the bathroom on the ledge. Some of those nests were used year after year so the outer edges were solid guano. I freshened up that cupola for a while at least.

Memories of the things I did make me wonder how I ever made it to my eighties without breaking my neck or at least some other bone in my body.

SKUNKS IN THE HOUSE

My first close encounter with skunks came at the age of seven. One spring, the hillside around a neighboring uncle's farm had an unusually high infestation of grub-worms, June bug larvae. To get those larvae, skunks dug up the sod, rolling it up in rolls like a sod farm harvest. Someone shot one of those skunks and the babies gathered around her in desperation. My cousins gathered the babes up but found the perfume repulsive and were told, "Get rid of those skunks. Buster will take them."

Four beautiful black and white baby skunks were delivered into my hands. They couldn't live in the house, but Bob and I had a sand-hole. The driveway went through a natural sand deposit. We had dug down through layers of pure sand, and had quite a hole. The idea was to dig a deep hole with straight sides so the skunks would be confined. It would be perfect for those baby skunks. It was their home.

While I was playing with them, I must have gotten too rough with one. It hit me on the chest with a little yellow droplet of perfume. The smell and effect of that little drop was immediate. Like an onion, it burned the eyes, and the smell was nothing at all like I associated with the smell after it had aged for a while. It was almost like tear gas.

That cleared me out of the sand hole. The skunks dug their way out of the sand trap during the night, and were on their own.

Years later, my son came home from grade school with five baby skunks he and his friends had found along the road. The little skunks were "oohed" and "ahed" over, and brought into the basement to a nice nest to keep them warm and confined. Old Sookie, our Siamese cat, would have nothing to do with them. They were very beautiful and cuddly. My wife tried to play with them until she also got the friendly warning right in the middle of her forehead. Scrubbing, special soap, tomato juice, the whole bit finally got rid of the smell, but that was it. Those skunks had to go.

We returned them to a wooded area where the habitat was to a skunks liking. Some veggies from our frig would provide some food. They went off in the woods in single file following the leader to lend their energy to controlling the beetle population in that forest.

SWALLOWS

That navy blue forked tail miniature jet skimming back and forth across the lawn was a swallow, a wonderful feathered mosquito eater; a barn swallow. In the summer, they were constantly swooping across the landscape in their quest for flying insects.

They nested in the barn right over the cows. I watched them twice a day while milking by hand. They were very trusting. Their family life unfolded before my eyes as I rhythmically squeezed those teats. From building the nest to feeding and caring for the hatchlings to taking the first flight as juveniles; it all happened right there over my head. Watching the home life of those birds fascinated and educated me while I was milking.

The swallows returned in April hungry after their long migration flight from South America. Nest building started by late May. After a rain they found mud of the right consistency, and mouthful by mouthful, pasted it to a beam where a nail or some other protrusion provided support. A wet tier of mud outlined each day's work as the nest took shape. It was completed, lined with fine chicken feathers, within a week. Watching them building the nest, setting the eggs, and later, feeding their newborn from birth to leaving the nest was a moving story.

Those feathered cement masons often played with a chicken feather brought to line the nest. They would drop it, then dive to catch it before it hit the ground. Occasionally there was competition between birds to see who could catch the falling feather. There never was a shortage of feathers because Mom had a hen house full of chickens.

Either parent incubated four or five eggs. After they hatched, whenever a parent flew near the nest, all the mouths opened wide begging. Those hatchlings were house trained. After a baby was fed, it backed up to the edge of the nest, and discharged a gelatin-encapsulated feces, which the parent grabbed and carried outside. The windows were always open for the continuous traffic as the parents brought in the meals, and left with the baby's excrement to fertilize some field. I wondered if they ever used that turd to bomb a car for fun.

The young grew quickly and soon spent a lot of time grooming their sprouting feathers, and later, hanging on the edge of the nest exercising their wing muscles. They were getting ready for that solo flight; the most critical event of their lives. Cats, crows, hawks and many other predators quickly grabbed any who were too weak to avoid capture. By this time it was risky to sit directly beneath those fledglings. The parents couldn't keep up with latrine duty.

The parents would not tolerate a cat. When one appeared there was a tremendous scolding. The nestlings hunkered down in the nest as the parents swooped and clicked their bills at the cat. Sometimes the cat leaped at them, but I never saw a swallow get caught.

The first fledgling to leave the nest almost seemed to be pushed into flight due to the sheer lack of space. After the first one left, the others plucked up courage, and gave it a try. They did come back to the nest the first night, but then were gone. The adults raised two or even three batches of young in a good season.

The swallows finished nesting in mid-summer. The rest of the season the young practiced their flying maneuvers becoming predators of the evasive ever-increasing insect population.

This time of year swallows were constantly diving in front of the lawn mower. I noticed some small millers flying desperately out of the grass to get out of the way when I was mowing the lawn. As a miller fluttered into the air, a swallow swooped down and the miller disappeared into that gaping mouth. That became my entertainment while mowing; watching those millers to see if they got back down in the grass before a swallow swooped by and caught them. Occasionally two swallows dove after the same miller. They never collided, but there were some near misses. When Dad was mowing hay, all the swallows in the neighborhood were constantly crisscrossing in front of the horses so close at times; they were in danger of colliding.

They were also constantly flying around a grazing herd of cattle. Anything that scared the insects into the air gave the swallows a chance to catch them.

It amazed me how the swallows could swoop down over water and just touch the surface with their bills. I assumed they were getting a drink but maybe they picked up an occasional insect, also.

I envied cousin, Edna. I couldn't figure why cliff swallows nested under the eaves on her barn, and not on mine. One year cliff swallows did start putting up their gourd shaped mud nests on the east side of the barn beneath the roof overhang. I blamed the sparrows for driving them away. They appropriated some of those nests actually using them as a birdhouse for their own nests.

The barn swallows with their forked tails were always a joy to watch; their flying maneuvers, their family life, and their trust of the farmer gave me a feeling of respect and admiration. I could understand this old proverb: "If you pull down an inhabited swallows nest your barn will burn down."

SENIOR CITIZEN

AFTER THE WAY IT WAS

CALLS FROM THE WILD

I woke up one night to a caterwauling cry in the trees a short distance from the house. I had a feeling that my cat, Lisa, had tangled with some coyotes I'd heard howling in that direction.

That summer, Lisa often stayed out late in those woods and must have been caught. I lay there assuming she was dead. Then the terrible racket started up again. "She's still alive!"

I jumped into my shoes, ran downstairs, out the front door, and sprinted towards the woods and the sound. A slight dip in the lawn didn't show in the shadow less moonlight, and I went sliding head first on the grass.

The sound kept coming from the woods, but, as I came closer, it stopped so I returned to the house. I glanced in the living room as I went up the stairs. There was Lisa, sound asleep on the carpet. What had I been chasing?

Again that week I heard the same sound. It was closer this time, and once more I went racing out the door. This time it stopped immediately so I couldn't place it, and I went back to bed.

Later that summer, some screech owls with their high-pitched cries were in the neighborhood. As I listened to them I got to thinking, do they have another call like the one I heard earlier in the woods? I bet they do. That's got to be what I heard!

Satisfied I'd solved my mystery, I quit worrying about Lisa staying out late in coyote territory. She had her own special way of getting in if we had gone to bed so she stayed out as long and as late as she wanted.

Somehow, she figured out she could climb the square corner of a box window facing the family room below our bedroom. From the little hip roof over that window, she jumped two feet to the attached garage roof protruding past the end of the house. Then she walked up over the peak and down to a window in our bedroom to scratch and tap on the glass or screen until we woke to let her in.

Sometime later, I had a message on my answering machine from a friend saying he had a baby owl in his garage. What should he do? I knew it couldn't be a baby. It was December. My guess was a screech owl. Before I got back to him, he had taken some pictures with his camcorder and let the owl go. It flew to a branch over his head where another owl flew down to it, and they both flew off together.

Later, we hooked his camcorder up to the TV, and compared his owl with the bird book. It looked like the screech owl, but he said he didn't think it had ear tufts. Reading the comments in the book, it said the screech owl was sometimes mistaken for the saw-whet owl, which did not have ear tufts. That's interesting.

While reading about the saw-whet owl, one statement caught my attention. "This owl's cry, most frequently heard during March and April, has a peculiar scraping and rasping quality which suggests the sound made by filing a large toothed saw."

Bingo! That's what had drawn me out of the house to save my Lisa from the coyotes. Two saw-whet owls were talking back and forth.

Probably I'll never hear another one again, but if I do, I'll sure listen with the picture of those saw-whets vocalizing, and me sliding across the grass while running to save my Lisa from those coyotes.

Imagination can make us see or hear things in such a way that we are sure it's what we want or fear it might be. Some saw-whet owls were calling each other that night. I mistook their call for my cat being captured and mauled by coyotes.

MY MONEY BELT EPISODE

The purpose of a money belt is to prevent money and valuables carried with you from being lost or stolen. My daughter-in-law strongly advised me to use one on my upcoming trip. I strapped mine on, and took off for Africa on the vacation of a lifetime. The pouch stuck out in front of me like a fungus growing on and old dead stump. I carried it with me wherever I went. That belt was an inconvenience, always in the way. My only worry was would I leave it in some bathroom when I removed it during my frequent visits.

I arrived in Cape Town, relieved to be on the ground. I cleared customs, and was on my way with my old friend, Peter, to four weeks of adventure.

The first trip started at a citrus orchard. The owners, Nita and Mike, ran a bed and breakfast for extra money to send their son to college. After our morning breakfast, they drove us to the Addo Elephant Preserve for our first safari. By noon, we had seen a variety of animals: desert tortoises, wart hogs, ostriches, various antelopes but no elephants. Nita had scheduled a "briea", or a midday barbecue, with a number of their friends—a wonderful introduction to life

110

in South Africa. I loaded up my plate, found a rock bench, and sat to enjoy lunch. The money belt pouch protruding in front of me competed with my plate for space on my lap. I pushed the pouch around to my side out of the way. Finished with lunch, our safari continued until time to return to the B & B. We hadn't seen one elephant on our first day in the Addo.

The landscape was covered with thick bush broken occasionally by grassy expanses where groups of zebra and impala grazed. The impala were nick named McDonalds. From the rear, their camouflage forms a perfect McDonald's 'M' logo.

I used to think I was a good animal spotter driving on the hi-way but Nita and Mike saw all kinds of animals I had difficulty seeing even when they were pointed out to me. Their markings and coloration were next to perfect camouflage.

Back at the B & B, Mike gave us a tour of their citrus orchard, recent plantings and the drip irrigation system. "*Elephantoms*", the book I was engrossed in, occupied the rest of my relax time.

The next morning, dressing for the continuation of the safari, I decided to leave the cursed money belt at the cabin. It would be safe there, and not constantly in the way. The driver picked us up for another tour of Addo on the way to the adjoining Scotia Preserve.

The Addo Preserve elephants were out in force this morning moving through the scrubland. In the distance they appeared as large grey boulders, their backs just visible over the bush. Their movement was the only thing identifying them from the boulders. Our driver realized the water hole we just passed was their destination so we returned to watch the behavior at the reservoir.

It was quite a sight; elephant families arriving from two directions, undisturbed by the proximity of the cars. Their pace picked up as each group got closer to the water. The families greeted each other like long separated friends, screaming hellos, entangling their trunks with kisses and hugs; a behavior not unlike our family reunions and homecomings.

We moved on to the Scoitia Preserve. It had, until recently, been a dairy farm. We joined a French group of girls, and a new driver with an open air Land Rover. It was fitted for viewing and picture taking in all kinds of weather. The side panels rolled up so it was all open air; a welcoming breeze cooled our faces.

Scoitia had a more rolling landscape than the Addo with a bigger variety of animals, and more rangeland where grazers were evident. Elephants were purposely excluded from this preserve to save the trees and bush vegetation. We saw a number of different animals: eagle owl, black rhino, giraffe, lion, and a variety of antelope.

We were entertained at lunch by a good harmonica player and the hostess who sang and played the guitar. At the end of the tour, a driver delivered us back to our citrus grove B & B. He got a real extravagant tip, I thought, simply because neither Peter nor I had anything smaller than 100 rand. I had a 20-dollar bill, and gave that to him. I figured out later, it would have been cheaper to give him the 100 R, as the exchange rate was about 6.4 R to the dollar.

Next morning was departure day. We got up for breakfast, and ate with two families of Norwegians with kids. Peter was in seventh heaven talking in Norse, and explaining where his family originated in Norway.

After breakfast it was packing time. I got all packed, but couldn't find my money belt. It was gone.

My whole African life was in that belt: cash, traveler's checks, plane tickets, and passport. We told Nita and Mike. They searched the room again, and the car. They assured us the maids were completely trustworthy. Where could it have disappeared?

Nita called the Addo park entrance facility where we had the briea; she knew the head lady there. Miracle of miracles, the belt was there. Not a thing was missing. Somebody up there likes me.

I don't know who was more relieved, but they would have to go some to beat the cloud I moved out from under. Later, Peter mentioned, he had been going over in his mind all we'd have had to go through just to replace my passport.

After that, I wore the money belt securely strapped around my waist except when we were at Peter's Sunny Cove Manor. There were no more belt episodes in Africa, but this is only half the story.

I got on the plane returning to the states with the money belt strapped firmly around my waist. My customs entry to the USA was the international terminal in Detroit. After clearing that, I passed through the security check to get to the American terminals removing everything metal: shoes, pocket contents, jackets, vests, watch, belt and of course, money belt into the x-ray trays. I passed through with no problem, redressed on the freedom side, and headed for the shuttle train to the American Airlines terminals.

I sat relaxing on a seat, and looked down at my waist. I suddenly realized the money pouch was not protruding in front of me. When the shuttle stopped I stayed on, and retraced my steps back to the security checkpoint. I found a lady officer who, when she heard my story, busily searched for my money belt. It was not around. She enlisted the help of another officer who looked at me, and asked what that dark belt was around my waist? It was the belt to which the pouch was attached—at the back of my waist. The lady gave me a big hug. I think she was almost as relieved as I was, but that would be hard to beat. I didn't have time to think about it. I had to get back on that shuttle to catch my flight to Chicago.

Lately, I blame a lot of things on getting old. This is one more thing I'm blaming on aging.

THE WATER HOLE

Picture a gently rolling, pastel pink landscape. Bisect this with eroded, dried up, rock strewn gullies. Cover it with leafless thorn bushes grabbing, snagging, tearing, clothing coming anywhere near, and you have South Africa's Kruger National Park in October. The impression was desert. A whole ecosystem of plants and animals live in this park. How they can survive is a mystery to this farm boy, but they do and have for ages.

The dry season was nearing its end. Everything was parched, shriveled, wilted; conserving what little moisture was available. Increasing numbers of creatures frequented the reservoirs still holding water. Local reservoirs had dried up forcing animals into longer distance travels for water.

My first morning's walking safari into this terrain made me wonder if I'd miscalculated my aged abilities. Every bush seemed to try to drag me in, and hold me with some kind of thorn. Most of them didn't want to let loose once they had me.

Game preserves maintained permanent animal populations with some form of constant water supply. The Addo Elephant Preserve did it with water pumped from wells into reservoirs. Kruger Park used dammed up streambeds, which filled with water during the wet season making a pond that lasted through the dry season. Chobe Preserve exploited a permanent river surrounding a large grassy island as its water source. Water was the main essential anchoring wildlife to a territory. Most animals needed water every day.

Bushes use every available form of thorn for protection. Many of the surviving animal species have adapted to use the bushes in spite of the sharp spines. Tourists suffered and learned to avoid the branches at all costs, especially after getting caught, and discovering fighting your way out doesn't work. You just get more tangled. One had to disengage slowly without touching another snag. Most of the bushes were a little more than head high.

Remains of trees elephants had pushed over to strip the bark were evidence of the destruction they are capable of to survive. A few large trunk trees either got too big before elephants got to them or were species repulsive to the pachyderms. Trees were sparse with evidence elephants harvested many by pushing them over and stripping the bark, in some cases digging up the roots to chew. They actively gouge the earth with their tusks, and dig the soil with their feet. Some places, they pulled out bushes, roots and all as forage.

The overall impression was everything is dry, but when it finally does rain, it comes down hard.

The Addo Wildlife Preserve was surrounded by a fence enclosure buried two to three feet in the ground and rising eight to ten feet above ground. That plus an electrified wire kept the animals in the preserve out of surrounding farms.

Safaris take advantage of watering holes to ensure tourists sight more animals. Our group routinely visited a water hole by a large earthen dam about two stories high. This formed a pond close to three acres in size about two hundred yards wide. It drew thirsty animals, large and small.

One evening just before sunset, we parked the Land Rover on top of the dam to enjoy our "sundowner" (drinks and snacks) while watching the sun go down. It was a beautiful sight even when there were no clouds in the sky.

A lone elephant appeared out of the bush walking to the water's edge to drink. He seemed to materialize out of nowhere. Even though they are the largest living land mammals on earth, they can move through the bush without making a sound.

Suddenly he wheeled facing our direction. The guide urgently whispered, "Everyone back in the Rover." You wouldn't believe how fast and silently we got back in that vehicle. The elephant stood alert a minute or two, and then relaxed turning to finish his drink. Our tracker thought a rhino had made the noise that startled him. One did appear, but he came from the opposite direction to what the elephant was facing. A full moon provided enough light to see the rhino move out of the bush, and down to the dried up stream bed about a hundred yards above the water hole.

The elephant, with his thirst quenched, moved to the muddy area at the head of the pond. He sloshed the mud and water around with his front feet until it was the right consistency to suck up in his trunk and spray over his back.

Unlike most of the other large animals in Africa, elephants use mud dried on their back to trap the annoying lice and ticks. When they rub off the dried mud, ticks and lice come along too. The ox pecker, a robin sized bird, does the job for most of the other large beasts. These birds feast on the blood filled parasites while catching a free ride.

All the while the elephant was mud bathing, the rhino patiently and silently waited. He was reluctant to associate with the elephant. The elephant, finally satisfied with his bath, moved on disappearing quietly into the bush.

The rhino had the area to himself. He stopped first at the mud bath. We could barely see him, but there was no mistaking when he got there. He laid down, let loose a tremendous fart and a long sigh of relief. His wait was worth it. Everyone laughed as we moved on to the campsite for our evening meal.

The male elephant is periodic in its breeding behavior. He is said to be in musth when actively seeking females in estrus, Musth is evidenced by mucous seepage from temporal glands on the sides of his head. Bulls in musth also leak urine and are unpredictable and extra dangerous.

Another day, we had a very unique experience with a bull elephant at the same water hole. We parked on the dam to watch a family drinking. While there, another family came out of the bush. The two families meeting behaved like a home coming among humans; trumpeting, engaging trunks, touching, rushing to say hello. A bull in musth was with one of the groups. Young bulls still with the matriarchal group tried their jousting techniques with the old bull, but there was never any contest. They were just sort of arm wrestling to see how strong the "old man" really was.

After the greetings, they all satisfied their thirst, and moved to the mud bath to finish that part of the ritual. The big bull had his own mud bath in the shallow middle of the pool. Finished, he came up the slope of the dam to the top as close as he could get to our vehicle. He could just reach his trunk over the top of the dam and lay it on the ground extended towards us. He could actually touch the tires on the Rover. He sniffed the people in the back, and immediately turned around and rubbed his rear on the rough gravelly embankment as if to say, "That's what I think of you."

Moving to the front end of the car he sniffed us out. I swear he had a twinkle in his eye. We met his approval so he left to finish his toilet with a dust bath in the bush up ahead. Our guide said he had never seen anything like that before. There never was any threat in the bull's behavior. He just seemed to give us the once over.

Baby elephants were miniature replicas of adults. No baby like features, just a trunk that needed lots of practice before it could be expertly maneuvered. Fortunately, suckling doesn't actively involve the trunk. Just get it out of the way. Aunts, sisters, young uncles, and brothers all showed their interest for a newborn member of the family. If the baby got in any kind of trouble, they were all ready to help.

At the Addo Elephant Preserve, a family moved towards the water reservoir. A youngster moved with the herd. As they neared the water the pace noticeably increased. When they got there the baby behaved like a kid at the end of a long car ride, running around curious and investigating.

A plover started dragging its wing and spreading its tail to draw the babe away from its nest. I saw the youngster stop with his ears out and trunk elevated in the typical charge position. He rushed at the plover, who having successfully drawn the juvenile away from her nest, flew away. The youngster stood there, ears wide with trunk proudly raised. He had saved the herd from this great danger in their path.

For me, the elephants were the most fascinating animals seen on this African adventure, both from the sightings and from the stories read and told. These animals were unique as well as curiously intelligent. It puzzles me, that having lived side by side with them for centuries, we still know so little about them. With all our studies and scientific monitoring systems, we still come up with new discoveries regularly.

Their communication system is just now beginning to be appreciated.

Their family life is matriarchal but leaves much to be revealed yet. The paternal side seems not to have been studied at all. Ivory, the source of much of the species harassment has inflicted a deep distrust of man. We have put pressure on the race to even survive in the wild.

MANURE SPREADERS

On the farm, we spent a lot of energy getting rid of the animal waste. That was the function of the manure spreader. It put the waste back on the land where it originated. There, it helped propagate chlorophyll to capture more energy. Pastured animals including wildlife are their own manure spreaders, no energy wasted in distribution.

After going on safari in Africa I had a much higher respect for manure and manure spreaders. In addition to being excellent fertilizer, manure and manure spreaders are accomplished storytellers. Each species had a distinct stool, their personal calling card, which not only identified them, but also told something about them; for one thing, their diet. The wildlife populations in parks gave away their presence and numbers with the dung they left along the trails. Each beast had a distinctive stool. Guides and trackers were expert in reading trail signs.

That stool identified what different animals ate. In the case of the civet cat, it explained how they could survive eating a large millipede containing lethal concentrations of cyanide. In addition to the millipedes, the civet devoured a woody diet that neutralized the cyanide. As a result the civet produced the biggest turd for body size of any animal in the forest. So if you want to call some bully "a big ass hole," just call him a civet cat and he's not likely to hammer you.

Nature makes use of most everything. Offal is not only fertilizer, for some animals it is a means of marking territory. Rhinos defecate on or near a bush and then kick the offal on to the bush as a sign this is their range. Urine is almost universal in its use on signposts denoting territorial boundaries and sexual condition. Our guide pointed out where a rhino had pooped and then kicked it on a bush. This alerted us to be on the lookout. That rhino might still be in the area.

A group of beetles use dung rolled into a ball to lay an egg in. They roll this ball of feces to some spot and bury it. Fermentation produces enough heat to hatch the egg. They were called dung beetles. They seemed to be especially attracted to elephant dung. We watched a dung beetle rolling a ball of dung much bigger than it was. It amused me seeing Mother Nature on the job making use of everything. The elephant diet consists of forage with large quantities of poorly digestible bark from tree trunks and roots. Their dung was very evident along the trails. It maintained the shape of the bowel it came from; about the size of a large can of chow mien.

Watch out when your guide picks up some dark, one-inch diameter hard stones and asks what you think they are. He'll say they are used in a native game in which you put them in your mouth and blow them as far as you can, even demonstrating for us. Don't join his game! It is giraffe dung. Don't worry. If you try it, you will survive.

The taste was bitter!

DOROTHY'S TREASURES

My late wife, Dorothy, loved her pieces of antiquity, especially Moorcroft and other china plus family silver. Watching the "Antiques Road Show" on Public Television stimulated that interest, and always brought the comment, "Why don't they come to Chicago? I'd like to know the value of some of these treasures." But she left this world never having that opportunity.

One day, flipping the channels, I perked up when I heard tickets to the Antiques Road Show were available for a $65 dollar donation to the public television's fund raising drive. Call this number.

This was her chance. I had to take it for her. A pleasant voice answered the phone. The tickets were going fast but she finally secured a pair. Each ticket was good for the appraisal of two items. I gave the required information and the Road Show adventure was under way.

Frances, our daughter-in-law, planned to visit in the summer. The road show was being filmed while she was in town. Shortly after she arrived, we got to work. The biggest problem was deciding which objects to take, and then finding them, since most items of supposed value had been put away when realtors were showing the house.

Dorothy had an old sampler she was curious about plus family silver and plenty of china. We found the china and silver but the sampler didn't turn up. Once we found the wooden Indian masks, we stopped looking. Some silver, china and four masks seemed to be a nice combination of things to take. Each treasure was carefully wrapped in newspaper and stuffed in a Styrofoam box. The relics were ready to go to the Chicago Road Show.

The morning of the show, I dressed in a blue pull over shirt and maroon pants. I asked if I looked all right. Frances, as politely as she could, said, "The shirt has food stains on it and the pants look like something from a rummage sale," which they were; so I changed to a short sleeve dress shirt and khaki pants.

We caught the 10 o'clock train to Chicago and via taxi, arrived at Navy Pier. We got in line for the road show just before noon. We finally reached the head of the line and were directed to the appraiser tables for our particular items. The American Indian line was the first we entered.

I placed the four wooden masks on the table, and the appraisers said nothing to us. When we tried to talk to them they said they weren't allowed to talk to us about the items. I wondered if I had something I wasn't supposed to have. I had heard or read about the Indians recovering from museums some of their antiquity taken surreptitiously. Finally they told us they were waiting for someone who was over at a table in another part of the room to come and look at our masks. I was still leery. We didn't know if this was good or bad. Maybe we had something that was illegal. They did offer us their chairs, which we appreciated. We had been standing for a long time, but they still said nothing to us.

One appraisal while we were sitting there was interesting. A collector came up to the table with a foam lined hinged leatherette box. He opened it and took out an Inca figurine, which they estimated at two hundred dollars. He was all upset saying it was worth much more than that. After he left, one appraiser remarked to the other one "That will be another letter of complaint. I have a number of those figurines in my shop and they sell for two hundred dollars each."

Finally, whomever we had been waiting for came. The masks were taken for inspection behind a screen. A lady came out and said she was the producer of the show and needed to know what I knew about the masks. "Only that my wife's father, while working as a forest ranger on the west coast of British Columbia, had been given the masks as a gift by the Indians." She asked, "Would it be alright if we film the appraisal?" "Of course!" I said, relieved.

Then she told us to follow a guide to the green room. They had some papers I signed and then they put on my make-up.

The green room was a space curtained off from the rest of the area. It had about a dozen tables to sit at with your antiquity. I remember someone had what looked like some kind of a big urn and another table had some kind of a picture or painting. I recall another table had some kind of bottles. Families sat around the tables, but only one person at a time went out to the filming. Two long tables sheltered the makeup area.

With the papers signed and my face powdered, we waited for the filming. We sat and looked at the other people waiting for their turn in the spotlight. Apparently we had just missed being served lunch because Frances found one sandwich left on a tray and grabbed it. We even had to get a ticket from one of the caretakers to go to the bathroom. I had to go twice so you see how long we waited.

There was a TV in each corner of the green room where the filming could be observed as it was going on. Frances would observe it from there since the noise was so loud in the filming area you couldn't hear what was being said.

It seemed like we waited for hours but finally we saw the appraiser from the Indian table come in and get his makeup treatment so it looked like it was getting close to show time.

The call came for Mauer so away I went with our wooden masks. The filming crew was very well organized. Someone got the masks pinned up on a display board while another got me and the appraiser wired for sound. It reminded me of bees running around attending the queen in a beehive.

Finally the director said they were going to test the system and she asked me if I had a dog.

"No, but I have four cats." Then she asked, "What are their names?" That caught me so far off guard, I rattled off four names, one of which was of a cat that died 20 years ago. Then she came over and whispered in my ear that the appraiser was a little hard of hearing. Could I speak a little louder? The way she did it, almost got me laughing.

She introduced the appraiser as an expert in the field of Indian artifacts. Then I introduce myself as Russell Mauer from Crystal Lake, Illinois and the show was on. He said he had been doing this show for eight years waiting for something like this and here it was. What did I know about the masks? Only that my wife's father was a forest ranger on the west coast of British Columbia and had been given these masks by the Indians.

He then proceeded to tell what he knew about the masks. The small masks were chief's masks worn attached to some headdress or hat tied by the three holes at the bottom and sides of the mask. They were worn for ceremonials and meetings. The big mask was used for ceremonial plays and held in front of the face. He thought they had been made in the late nineteenth or early twentieth century. He knew the name of the tribe that made these masks, the Kwakwaka'wakw. They were from the Alert Bay area on Vancouver Island, British Columbia.

Sometime in the past, I remember my wife mentioning Alert Bay and that she even played with the Indian children.

Then came the question, "Do you have any idea what these are worth?"

"Not the slightest."

"The big mask is worth between twenty-two and twenty-five thousand dollars, the beaver mask between eight and ten thousand, while the other two are between ten and twelve thousand each. What do you think of that?"

Figuring that required some kind of a superlative, I said, "WOW!!!"

They needed more filler which they somehow communicated to the appraiser so after a few seconds looking at each other, he started telling about these masks being owned by individual chiefs and therefore it was legal for someone to be given these articles. If the tribe had owned them I would have had to give them back to the tribe.

That completed the filming. Frances came running out of the green room and almost bowled me over with a big hug. We packed up the masks and quickly got put in the front of the line for our silver and china appraisals. We were so high after that I don't even remember what they were appraised at. I think between twenty-five and two hundred fifty dollars covered it.

We rewrapped everything, and very carefully packed it back in that Styrofoam box and caught a taxi back to the train depot. Of course we went to the wrong station and spent a good hour finding the Metro station supposedly in the next block.

After getting something to eat, Frances called Dave, Dorothy's son, back in Raleigh. His comment after hearing the news was, "That is some expensive kindling."

THE BLACK BANTAMS

The sixth grade science project in my son's school one year was hatching some chicken eggs. The project was over when the eggs hatched so the baby chicks were fostered out to receptive kids who brought them home to surprised parents. Our downy black chick immediately became one of the family, sandwiched between episodes with a family of skunks and a young red tailed hawk supposedly destined to be a falconer's prize raptor.

The chick, in the first day of its life, was still in its impressionable age. Our old Siamese cat, Sookie, had the misfortune of being around the chick that first day enough that it imprinted on her. Fortunately for the chick, Sookie was a non-aggressive very tolerant ten-year-old feline with no inclination toward a fresh rather than a canned dinner. Unfortunately for Sookie, that chick was bound it would not let her out of its sight. It followed her everywhere. If Sookie lost the chick for a minute, it would run around frantically searching until it found her. The cat, in desperation, would try to hide under the bureau, but the chick would find her, crawl up on her, scratch out a nest in her fur and go to sleep. I'm amazed old Sookie would tolerate that, but maybe it had something to do with the way, years earlier, she started life with our family.

We purchased Sookie at weaning. Within a week she was packed in the car for a long trip from Washington State to northern Minnesota where she became a de-facto mascot for all the teenage employees of our A&W root beer stand. The trip made her partial to cars while the exposure to the teenagers saddled her with a very gregarious personality.

The chick grew very fast sprouting shiny black feathers becoming a full-fledged bantam pullet. Sookie and the pullet were always together although the bantam didn't sit on her anymore. They both lived in the house. The pullet enjoyed riding in cars as long as Sookie was along.

The pullet never developed normal roosting behavior even after she got all her feathers and could fly. She was always put in a box at night to sit on an old cashmere sweater. This sweater probably reminded her of Sookie's fur so she slept quite content with the box covered to keep her warm and confined. This was her bedtime roost all her life. She never did learn to sleep on a perch.

Sometimes when I came home from work and sat down to relax in front of the TV, the pullet would get up on my shoulder. She'd cackle away in chicken talk to the point I had to put her in her box and cover it. That was the only way to get her to shut up. I had my wife to talk to, and it didn't take long to have enough of the pullet's description of her day.

Vacation, the year of the bantam, was a trip from North Chicago to a lake near Moorhead, Minnesota. We pulled a pop-up camper trailer. Sookie and the bantam went along. The bantam was right at home in the car as long as Sookie was there. They sat in the back window together drawing second looks from motorists passing us on the interstate. At the lake, chicken and cat were part of the scene going and coming as they pleased. To our friends, this was a strange combination, but they knew Sookie from ten years ago at the root beer stand, and they were also animal lovers so they enjoyed the company. Sookie and the pullet often went off in the woods around the lake, but they always found their way back. I never did try to take them out on the lake though.

Back home in Illinois, neighbor Al, who had a few leghorn chickens of his own, thought it was criminal to raise that black bantam pullet without a mate. One day at a trade fair, Al found a black bantam rooster. It was one of those with feathery black pantaloons clear down over its toes. It was a present for our pullet.

He was quite the rooster, always trying to lord it over the pullet. She really didn't think much of him, just staying close to Sookie most of the time. The rooster didn't trust that old Siamese cat, so he never got very close to the pullet. At least they didn't fight.

Within a week after the rooster arrived the pullet was dead. The pullet lay dead in the middle of the floor one day when we returned from shopping. It was like she'd had a heart attack. She had probably picked up some disease from the rooster to which she had no resistance, having never seen another chicken. It was very acute in its effect resulting in a heart attack like death.

This was like a death in the family. Even old Sookie missed the pullet, mopping around sort of looking for her. The family survived, but now there was a single bantam ruling the roost again. He'd sit on a shelf looking out the window while in the house. Outside where he spent most of the day, he'd chase grasshoppers and scratch up snacks in the grass. In the evening he was at the door to be let in. The bathroom was his chosen spot to roost. He'd fuss and fume at the door until we opened it. Then up on the counter where he'd settle in for the night.

One morning just after I left for work, Dorothy glanced out the front window just as a red fox ran out of the garage with her black bantam rooster in his mouth. She ran out the back door to intercept him. Her shouting and screaming apparently so surprised him that he opened his mouth and the bantam dropped out and ran off. Then the fox started coming towards her. She picked up sticks and threw them at the fox as she gradually made her way to a neighbor's house.

The bantam had also made it to the neighbor's house and was hiding behind a hedge. In spite of the neighbor's warnings, Dorothy ran back out and got the bantam. He was in so much shock his comb was almost black. He didn't even try to get away from her. She put him in their garage out of harm's way. Another neighbor got his gun, and shot the fox still circling the neighborhood. We had him tested for rabies. The result was negative which was a relief.

The fox may have been raised for part of its life in a home so it didn't have the usual fear of humans. More than likely, it had a family of half grown pups and was taking the rooster to train them in capturing and killing prey. Ordinarily, with one bite it would have dispatched the chicken so it would have been dead the minute it was caught. This method of training, bringing live prey back to the young, is a training method used by many canines.

The poverty poker club met at my house one evening that summer. The room we met in was also the one the rooster roosted in on a shelf occasionally. Our game didn't deter him from the shelf even though there was lots of noise and light, but as the night advanced the smoke got to him. He was pretty distressed. He tried to get his head out of the room by reaching it around the corner. He finally got down and demanded to be let in the bathroom. The smoke was too much for him. Lung cancer wasn't the way to go for a rooster who had survived the jaws of a fox.

Shortly after that we convinced neighbor Al to take the rooster back to his hen yard. It was fox proof and with that harem of leghorn hens to boss around, he would live out his life free from any predators or smoke, and be ready for his roost every evening.

OSCAR THE SQUIRREL
I was his tree

Oscar, the squirrel, came to our house after a road kill disaster. His mother crossed the street without allowing for the speed of an auto. When she saw the vehicle, she was halfway across and decided to turn back. That was fatal. The hungry Oscar left the nest to search for anything that might satisfy his thirst and hunger. He hadn't been out of the nest enough to know how to find his way back so when night fell, he was still out on a limb. That night it rained with a high wind. As a result, Oscar was shaken from his branch and ended up in the grass by the sidewalk.

Dorothy, coming to work in the morning, found him wet and shivering in the grass by the gate. All she had to feed him were some yellow grapes, which she sliced and offered to him. After a few protesting growls at being disturbed, he grabbed the slice with his paws, sucked the juice out of it, and began to nibble away at the pulp. Hoping that his mother would return, Dorothy covered him with some grass to keep him warm and left him alone. He was still there at the end of the day so she took him home to our house in the suburbs.

This was a strange new place for a baby squirrel. He needed something to eat and a place to sleep. An old syringe with warm milk substituted for a nipple. He sucked up the milk as it was slowly pushed out of the syringe. Watermelon was on the menu that evening so we gave him a thin slice. He grabbed the slice with both paws and sucked the juice out of it like he'd been doing that all his life. Finished with the juice, he nibbled the remaining pulp like it was his dessert.

The cats had been warned not to molest or hurt Oscar. Tigger with no front claws was the first to investigate. When Oscar approached, she ran. That was her mistake. He chased and he had her buffaloed. Soon Lisa became curious and also retreated when he advanced so he had both of them spooked. Tom was a mouse and gopher eater so he was a worry to us. A shout was enough to make him avoid Oscar when he first saw him. Now Oscar was king of the hill. Chasing soon became part of his territorial protection policy. Even humans were subject to his aggressive behavior. People were subjected to a scratching attack but only if Oscar was resting on me.

Oscar needed a nest to sleep in. We never used the Jacuzzi. That could be his home. I put an old heating pad wrapped in a towel with another towel over it in a cardboard box. That made a warm nest for him in the tub. Before we had finished our dinner, he was asleep for the night under the towel. With the bathroom door closed, we were also assured that the cats would not make a meal of him before morning.

After a day of trying to keep him watered with the syringe, it was obvious there had to be a better way. A search at the pet store turned up a hamster-watering bottle, one of those with a ball bearing in the end of a spout that releases water when the bearing is pushed. He had to learn to use it, but that was not a problem. His approach to everything was, could he chew it? One bite on that ball bearing and water appeared. Now he had a watering hole whenever he wanted it. In a few days his bedtime routine started with the rattling of that ball bearing as he quenched his thirst. That, followed by silence, meant he had burrowed into his nest and was out for the night.

It didn't take long to find most clothing made excellent climbing, and shoulders made perfect perches. He wasn't used to climbing at first, but a few runs up and down a pant leg and he knew what he was made for. Soon it became a game for him to hang with his front paws free. "See how good I am at eating a nut while swinging free in the air."

The Jacuzzi was very slippery so it was effectively a prison until a towel hung over the rim anchored with a weight made a ladder, in and out, he could maneuver. Then the exploring started. There were still a lot of obstacles he couldn't negotiate but the old curiosity was there. Soon the rim of the tub was home territory; not too near the edge though. A couple slips into the tub, and he knew that he had to be careful. The monstrous steps down from outside the tub also resulted in some falls, but it was soon evident that those hind legs with their claws held perfectly on the wooden trim. He could hang over the edge and just reach the step below. For a while getting back was via the towel ladder, but he soon found he could reach up with his front paws and pull himself up to the rim. After that he didn't need that outside ladder, but he always needed the help of the inside ladder to get out.

Sweet corn was in season. A cross section of an ear cut the size of a checker was a delicacy. He would grab it like a harmonica and chew off the kernels as he quickly turned it around with his paws. One thing was evident from the beginning. If you're full, don't throw it away, cache it or hide it away for leaner days. It was evident an instinct was involved. Bury it even if you're on solid tile. Stuff it in and pull something over it.

Runs outside in a small cherry tree were fun, but somehow he seemed to prefer the flowerbed under the tree. That seemed to be more interesting to him. Maybe he still had memories of a rainy night and swaying branches in a big maple. He seemed to have a wonderful time digging in the dirt under the flowers, and if his dinner included more cashews than he could eat, that was a wonderful place to bury them. That soft soil meant he could dig a real hole, and properly cover it with nose tamping and all.

The pant leg and shoulder soon became home, and relaxation required some games. Tag was the game of choice with me always it. "Catch me if you can." He would zigzag even better than any football scat-back. Around and around my shirt he'd go. Then a cloth-covered chair became part of his territory. That was a real playground. Up, down, around, backwards, forwards, then a rest on the back of the chair for a short recovery period. Outside he also practiced maneuvers on the lawn darting back and forth, even flipping over on his tail once in a while.

Climbing seemed to be enjoyed more on the brick walls of our house than on our Japanese plum tree. He liked to hang by his hind legs anywhere his claws got a slight hold. Then he'd swing with his front legs free almost as if he were showing off. He discovered the California stone front of our fireplace was also something to climb. The wooden mantel half way up was very chewable plus it made a perfect observation deck. He dug a flower out of a pot at the end of the mantel. The pot was in a vase so I removed the pot leaving the vase. That vase was just the right size for him to curl up and sleep in. He found a paper towel, and somehow, dragging it between his front legs, got it up on the mantel and into that vase. Now he had his perfect nest. When he curled up in that vase no one could see him. Awakened from his nap, he would peek over the edge squinting like an old man coming into bright sun light from the dark. Then he'd duck back, curl up under his tail and go back to sleep.

Getting up on the dinner table was forbidden, but that didn't register with Oscar. When he figured out he could jump from chair to chair, he moved around the table from lap to lap or chair to chair. When no one was looking, he was up on the table, and then off when he was discovered. It was also a temptation to jump to the kitchen counter from a shoulder. That always resulted in a grab by some hand whisking him back up to a shoulder.

His destruction of property by chewing required the construction of a cage. When completed it was a wire mesh three-foot cube with a twelve-inch square door. We had a cat scratching post with a platform top he liked to play on so that went inside to make it feel more like home. Cashews on the platform on the post would keep his attention for a while so in he went. He tired of the cashews after a few minutes and began to investigate. Immediately, he realized he was trapped. The door was wedged shut and in less than five minutes he had it pushed open and was out. He hated the inside of that cage from then on. He climbed around the outside, and the cage top was one of his favorite eating-places, but inside was an insult. With a proper latch we could keep him inside the cage but he was so miserable we just left him outside and dismantled the cage.

When the family went on drives, Oscar went along too. Things might be in quite a mess if he were left alone too long in the house. His first time in the car, he went inside my vest and I got into the car.

When he peeked out he was in a strange place. Initially, he stayed right with the familiar vest but soon he was on the seat headrest. It was a good climbing post just like the family room chair. The puffy vest collar at the back of my neck made a perfect nest for a drowsy squirrel. It didn't take much driving to make him go to sleep.

Driving on short trips to the market was no problem. He just stayed in the car doing some exploring until he got tired, and then he'd climb up on the back of the seat and take his siesta. The bad part was his teeth. The steering wheel soon showed evidence of his skill at carving.

In the parking lot at the grocery store, a lady stopped to tell me I had an inquisitive accidental new passenger. When Oscar crawled up on my collar and made himself at home, she thought it was delightful. Another grocery store encounter led to the tale of a lady's adventures with a whole nest of baby squirrels orphaned by their mother's road accident. When the lady reached in to pet Oscar, he was ready to attack her. He wouldn't tolerate his territory being invaded by some stranger.

An outing to some wilderness property was interesting. We put him on a tree in the forest. At first he didn't seem to like it. After a bit he started to explore a little. Then we wanted to go pick some apples we had on the lot. It took some coaxing, but he finally came down to his favorite perch on my vest collar. The apple trees were in tall grass, and before we knew it, he had disappeared. He reappeared up a neighbor's tree. It took quite a bit of coaxing, but finally he came down to the old vest collar again. But after one more retrieval from the trees, we decided we'd better leave for home. If he disappeared again, we might have to leave him. It was getting dark, and he wasn't old enough to survive on his own, especially in unfamiliar territory with no one to put out food for him. He was so tired he slept the whole 150 miles home.

Oscar's introduction to farm life was enlightening for both of us. One day he went along with me on a farm job. When the job was finished, I opened the back of the van to put my equipment away. Oscar jumped out to investigate. A hungry farm cat was after him in a flash. It was a real chase. The cat almost had him a few times, but his evasion maneuvers that he had been practicing on the lawn kept him just out of reach of her claws.

It was a demonstration of how squirrels survive when being pursued by predators. That football scat-back again would have been envious of his moves. The farmer finally drove the cat off, and then we had the problem of catching Oscar. He wasn't about to let us get close to him. We finally drove him into a machine shop where, with the door closed, he was trapped. But he wasn't going to be caught if he could help it. He went back and forth, under machinery, into a corner and past his pursuers. Finally, the farmer, who had leather gloves on, caught him and quickly stuffed him inside my vest. Amazingly, once inside my vest, he was perfectly calm. That was his hollow tree; his safe haven.

Almost every day, Oscar would have a game by himself on the lawn. He would dart this way and that so quickly it was hard to imagine how he could change directions so fast. Occasionally he even flipped on his back, and then on his feet again. Although there was a tree in the yard, it never seemed to be involved in these games.

Oscar didn't vocalize very much. The first day or two when he was awakened from a sound sleep; he would make a sort of complaining growl, a protest at being disturbed. As he grew and became more territorial, he learned to scratch under the bathroom door to get us to let him out, but no vocalizing. One morning there was a terrible scolding outside. When we looked out the front door, there was Oscar up the brick garage wall hanging by his hind legs with his tail flipping angrily over his back. He was really disturbed, but there was no potential enemy visible. Maybe a hawk had flown over. My appearance silenced him, but he wasn't very anxious to come down.

Oscar's front paws were very interesting. When fully opened they work very efficiently for climbing trees. For holding something to eat though the very long fingers were folded into the palm of the hand so only one knuckle was showing. The equivalent of the human thumb was only a nubbin, but it seemed to be very important in holding and manipulating whatever was being eaten. The nut was held between these two crude paddles made when the fingers were folded into the palm of the hand. He rolled the nut around and around between those two paddles until it was in the proper position for chewing and nibbling. The vestigial thumb almost looked like it had accidentally been bitten off while chewing a nut. The hind foot had five long digits compared to the four plus a nubbin thumb on the front paw.

Black walnuts began to drop from roadside walnut trees as we got into the fall season. They had a tremendous husk, which got black and rotten after lying on the ground for a while. I picked up some of these, and smashed them with a hammer. Oscar considered this a real delicacy. He manipulated it around and around in his paws until that nut was positioned just right for his teeth to scoop out the meat. Those teeth could scoop out a half walnut shell so clean you would think a dentist's pick had been used on it. I think my cracking the shell for him spoiled him. I never saw him even attempt to gnaw an unopened shell even if the husk had been removed for him. Maybe they were just too hard or his teeth were not mature enough for that job yet. He sure liked that meat inside the shell though.

Oscar started going off in the woods near the house staying away longer and longer. Sometimes he was gone over night coming back for food occasionally. Finally he stayed away for a week, and we thought he'd finally gone back to the wild.

One rainy drizzly day, we heard scratching at the sliding glass doors. There were two squirrels out there on the deck. We opened the door and Oscar came in, but the other one stayed back at the edge of the porch. Oscar ran to his perch on the mantel, and got dried off and had his fill of cashews. Then he left, and we never saw him again. We feel he fully adapted to the wild with a mate, and will be around with his babes next year.

OVER THE EDGE

Luring toward the future,
the edge of beyond is before us.
The future is new horizons,
always advancing from us.
The way may be tortured and tenuous,
but follow, indeed, we must.
Others will somehow pursue
the track made with our dust.
The road map is individual,
a path for each to follow.
The end is a virtual blank,
pray to your Apollo.
Advice comes freely given
challenging to dissect.
Assistance if required,
difficult to accept.
Reason and faith may be opposites,
'whatever works' will serve.
Good luck and God's speed to all,
meet you beyond the curve.

EPILOGUE
From Scythe to Satellite

The way it was as a child growing up on a farm during the depression of the 30's is the theme of the first part of this book. The second part, using stories from my senior life, portrays the way it has become.

The end is not in sight, nor is it getting farther away. As I told my granddaughter in a dream, I won't leave her a fortune unless I forgo spending it all. Some of the way my life has become is in keeping with that statement.

Nature was a brilliant teacher for my brother and I as we grew up. We learned the ebb and flow of the land—not by studying it but by living it. Nettles stung, mosquitoes and deer flies bit and skunk cabbage stunk. Red-tailed hawks orbited the sky, wary rodents scurried for cover, and robins and bluebirds signaled spring's arrival while starlings and sparrows invaded the songbird's space. Looking back, my childhood seems close to perfect.

A farm-life upbringing led in two directions for my brother and me. He became a cabinetmaker and I, an embryo manipulator.

Our youthful days are gone, not the youth but the times. Today, modern machinery and methods make harvesting nearly a one-man operation, with little time for chasing butterflies, watching swallows or harassing sparrows. Chickens and eggs are big business with limited opportunity to study animal behavior, life's mystique, or what it's all about. The technical changes over the last century have led to an exponential change in the manner of things.

Childhood memories are still being recalled as being some of the greatest times of my life.

ABOUT THE AUTHOR

Russell Mauer was born in Mauston, Wisconsin in 1929. After two years in the Army as a lab tech, he completed a PhD in Animal Science Reproductive Physiology. Ten years of research at Abbott Lab and 30 plus years of commercial embryo transfer preceded retirement in 2007.

ABOUT THE BOOK

Fertile Clay and Attic Dust records my memories of growing up on a dairy farm in central Wisconsin. Recollections are mixed with present day impressions shaped by my liberal arts education. When I have felt my recalls to be unreliable, clouded by old age and dulled by a waning imagination, I have leaned on the memories of relatives and friends.

The strongest memories are of fishing in the trout stream, Brewer's creek, which ran through our farm. Swallows, sparrows, and chickens, along with varied livestock, all made their impressions. Farm machinery was constantly improving, increasing the efficiency of the agricultural business that never lost its drudgery. Depression and war years were seen as "the way it was".

My parent's generation saw very little of the world beyond their insulated community. Now in my senior years, I profit from the touring industry, which allows me to experience "the way" of other peoples and cultures.